THE BOY
WITH
MY FACE

Joy Wodhams

Copyright © 2021
JoyWodhams

All rights reserved

ISBN: 9798502037990

DEDICATION

A very special Thank You!

Over the past seven years I have written and published thirteen books for adults and children. THE BOY WITH MY FACE is my fourteenth – and my seventh for children.

As its story was nearing completion I decided, for the first time ever, to post an online invitation for keen young book lovers to read and comment on the manuscript. I asked for four readers, two boys and two girls aged 11 to 13 years, and eight responded, the youngest not yet ten!

I have loved the experience (which has been online only, mainly because of lockdown problems, and none of the readers were previously known to me), and I've been amazed by the maturity of these young people, the depth of their understanding and the intelligence of their comments. I'm pleased to say they all enjoyed The Boy With My Face as much as I enjoyed writing it!

With their permission I'm including their names (and ages) on this page.

Lacey Alderton	(Girl 13)
Harry Cantellow	(Boy 10)
Alicja Oparka	(Girl 11)
Isaac Boorman	(Boy 10)
Darcy Drury	(Girl 10)
William Allpress	(Boy 11)
Millie Randall	(Girl 13
Connor Yates	(Boy 11)

ABOUT THE AUTHOR

Joy Wodhams is descended from five generations of circus and theatre performers, artists, musicians and composers. She herself is a writer and artist, although most of the other genes have missed her out.

Several of her books for adults and children are set in her birthplace, Liverpool, UK, and one (THE BOY WHO COULD FLY) was inspired by her most famous ancester, a trapeze artist who met his tragic death whilst performing in 1891 You can read an extract at the end of this book.

OTHER PAPERBACKS AND E-BOOKS BY JOY WODHAMS

For Children and Young Adults:

The Mystery Of Craven Manor

The Boy Who Could Fly

The Girl In The Attic

Cabbage Boy

There's A Lion In My Bed!

The Family On Pineapple Island

For Adults:

The Reluctant Bride

Me, Dingo and Sibelius

Affair With An Angel

Never Sleep With A Neighbour

Short Story Collections:

The Floater

The Girl At Table Nine

Creative Writing:

How To Write Fiction

ONE

Ryan
He was not going to cry. Not any more. His Mum was gone and nothing could bring her back. Now he had to look after himself. He listened to the sounds of Joe stumbling around the kitchen, the clatter of dishes, a chair crashing over. Then the footsteps on the stairs.

He held his breath but the footsteps carried on past his door to the room Joe had shared with the boy's mother. Through the thin wall he heard Joe prepare for bed. Then came the snoring. And then the silence.

He waited. Half an hour. An hour. And then he crept out of bed. Already fully dressed under the duvet, he had only to pick up his rucksack and his boots.

He knew every step of the staircase, which ones creaked or groaned, and he took his time to reach the hall, to open the front door, to close it silently behind him and to tiptoe down the darkened street.

From a bedroom window of the house next door his friend Melanie watched him leave.

'Don't go,' she pleaded silently, as she had pleaded with him several times over the past few days. 'Let me help you.'

But how could she help? She was just a girl. Even her mother couldn't help. 'It's not our business,' she had said. 'Those two will find their own way. Sooner or later.'

Melanie stayed at the window until Ryan's dwindling figure turned the corner of the street. Even then she waited. Perhaps he'll turn back, she thought. She hoped. But another half an hour passed and the street remained empty.

The park was scary in the dark, silent except for the occasional sleepy cheep of a bird or the scurrying of unseen small animals. A bat flew low across his path, startling him, its wings so close they ruffled his hair.

Which path to take? He decided to head for the cafe. It would be closed, of course, but perhaps he could find somewhere nearby to shelter until it re-opened in the morning. Although it was still the middle of the night, he was hungry. All he had been able to find in the kitchen back home were a few squishy tomatoes, some cheese with green mould on its edges and some dried up slices of white bread. He had made a sandwich, but it was only to be eaten if he couldn't get anything else.

The cafe had a canopy roof above its entrance. He huddled beneath it, pulling the hood of his jacket close around his face, and tried to sleep, but sleep was impossible. Perhaps he should go back. But life at home had ended the day his mother died. Joe had never really wanted him, had only tolerated him because he and Mum had come as a package.

'If you want me, you have to take my son as well,'

she had said when Joe first came on the scene five years ago, and Joe had to agree.

And things had been OK at first, although not the same as for the kids in the street who had their real dads. Joe never took him to football matches, never helped with his homework, never chose his birthday or Christmas presents, never talked to him about school or what he wanted to do with his life. He left all that to Mum.

But now – now she was gone, and everything had changed. The house was filthy, Joe was drinking heavily and had lost his job, there was no food, no money – even the television had been sold. And then the blows had started. The first time, Joe had apologised. But only that first time. After that, whenever he had spent the evening at the pub – which was almost every evening – he would come home and start complaining. About anything and everything. If Ryan was already asleep, Joe would stagger up the stairs, rip back the duvet and yank him out of bed. And then the blows would start. The boy could stay there no longer.

He peered at the luminous fingers on the watch his Mum had given him for his thirteenth birthday. Another four hours before the cafe opened. If only he could sleep, but he was too wired, too fearful, too sad.

He opened his rucksack and began to finger through the few possessions he had packed. The photo of Mum, tucked carefully inside a folded sweater, his phone, the handful of coins and the single £5 note he had found hiding behind the cereal packets in the kitchen. Not much to start a new life. Perhaps he was crazy even to think of it. He imagined creeping back into the house, creeping back into his bed and pretending to sleep. Joe wouldn't be awake for hours yet. But no. Anything was better than a life with Joe and without his Mum.

At last his eyes closed and he slept.

He awoke to a foot nudging his shoulder and a voice above him.

'Who's this, then? Running from the police, are you?'

He stared up at the woman. Plump, middle aged, frowning, but not angry, he thought.

'No, I – I couldn't stay home, but – I've nowhere else to go.'

'Had an argument with your Mum, have you?' The woman shook her head. 'She'll be going spare, wondering where you are. Go home, lad.'

'I can't. She – she died. Three months ago, and – and I –.' No, he couldn't cry now. He stumbled to his feet, grabbed his rucksack. 'I'll go.'

But the woman's face had softened. 'Better have some breakfast first, hadn't you? Come on, you can have some of yesterday's leftovers.'

Inside, she turned on lights, started up urns and coffee machines and a toaster, and piled a plate high with sandwiches and pastries. 'Hot tea on its way,' she said. 'Eat up, then, and I'll pack some in a bag for you to take away, but you'll have to be gone before my boss gets here.'

Bolting down the food, he wished he could stay in the cafe forever, with this kind, friendly woman. Maybe even go home with her. But it was not to be.

Soon, she returned with a bag packed with more leftovers.

'Best if you don't come back,' she said. 'Go home. Anything's better than living on the streets.'

He felt tears pricking the backs of his eyes. She was wrong. There were worse things.

'What's your name?' she called, as he reached the door.

He didn't want to tell her. What if Joe came looking for him? But she smiled, and she'd been kind, giving him all that food.

'Ryan.' he said.

TWO

Simon

'Keep still, won't you?'

I'd thought it would be easy, sketching the cow in a fenced-off section of the barn, but I'd been trying for the past twenty minutes and still hadn't got anything decent. I was using charcoal and had already rubbed out the stupid animal's pose several times.

Out in the fields the cows seemed happy just to hang around and ruminate, or to bend their heads and crop the grass. But this one, here in the barn, just wouldn't keep still. Shifting from leg to leg, then lying down in the straw, then up again and staring at me with those big fringed eyes.

I closed my sketchbook. Perhaps I'd try a landscape instead. But then I saw something emerging from the cow's backside. It looked like a pale balloon.

'Oh! Gross!' I backed away. 'Mum!' I yelled. 'There's something wrong with this cow!'

But Mum didn't come. Instead I got Lissie. She's my Mum's partner's daughter and a pest.

'Good,' she said. 'I was hoping I wouldn't miss it. This is her first baby.'

I turned away. 'I don't want to see this.'

'Aren't you doing Biology at school? This'll be something to tell the teacher when you go back.'

I tried not to watch, but couldn't resist peeping. The cow was lying down now. The balloon thing had split and a small head and two front hooves had emerged. And then, suddenly, the rest of the calf slipped out and Lissie was there, rubbing it with straw and placing it beside its mother.

'Is that how –?'

'Human babies are born? Wow, you're really ignorant, aren't you?' she crowed.

Of course I knew how babies are born, but – balloons?

Lissie's lived on the farm most of her life and probably seen cows and sheep and chickens being born practically every day. Right now she's got that look on her face that says, *See, I may be two years younger than you but I know lots of things that you don't.* Well, who cares? She's got her life and she's welcome to it. One day I'll have my own life back, and see who crows then.

I took another peep. Gross, I thought again. Of course we had Biology lessons at school, but it wasn't the same as actually watching something – and with a girl right there as well.

I got away as soon as I could, leaving Lissie to coo over the cow and her calf.

In the house I picked up the newspaper from the letter box and took it up to my room. It was one of those local things, with never anything of interest in it. I was about to take it back downstairs when I saw the photograph. A boy who'd run away from home eight days ago. The police were asking for information from anyone who'd seen him.

I couldn't stop staring at the boy's face. It was only a photograph and the definition was poor, but . . . it was *my* face! The hair was different. I'd grown mine to match the others in my form at the new school. Long and floppy on top, short at the sides. This boy had cropped hair, no style to it. But everything else – the eyes, the nose, the mouth . . . I grabbed my sketchbook and some charcoal and began to sketch him. He was smiling in the photograph. I glanced into the mirror over my desk and smiled. Yes, the same. And then I gave him my hair style.

I tore the page from my sketchbook, pinned it to my noticeboard and stepped back. Yes. It could have been me.

'Knock, knock!'

It was Mum. She always knocked but never waited for me to invite her in. I grabbed the newspaper and shoved it under my pillow.

She glanced around the room. 'I'm putting the machine on. Any washing? Your bed could do with changing.' She moved towards it.

'I'll do it. I'll bring everything down,' I said quickly.

She raised an eyebrow. I know she thought I hid things from her, but usually I didn't. Not until today.

As she was leaving, she saw the drawing on my noticeboard.

'Self portrait – that's brilliant. You're such a good artist, Simon. You take after -' She stopped.

'My father? You never talk about him.'

'It's all in the past. We were just kids. Only a few years older than you.'

'I wish you had a photo of him. Perhaps we could trace him and find a picture of him now - '

'No, Simon. I don't even want to think about him, and neither should you. You've got me, you'll always have me – and now you've got Philip and Lissie as well -'

At the door she paused. 'You know, Simon, there's no reason why you couldn't combine your art with farming.' She waved towards the window. 'Don't you think this is wonderful?'

I was silent. What could I say? Too many things were changing in my life. Philip and Mum have only been together six months. They met when Mum came back to Liverpool for my grandfather's funeral and to sort out the house he'd left her. I didn't come with her then. I'd never met my grandfather, didn't even know I had one until he died.

Mum's name is Caroline, but Philip calls her Carrie. She and Philip are all lovey-dovey and they're planning to marry in the autumn, and that will make him my official stepfather and Lissie my stepsister, and we'll all live here forever. Mum is loving it all, but no-one's considered me. I don't want the farm, I don't want my new school – a boarding school, the one Philip had attended when he was a boy, I don't want to live out in the country, with nothing around but empty lanes and fields. And I don't want a new family.

I want my old life, back in London, just me and

Mum, and my mates.

After she'd gone I rescued the newspaper from the bed and took out the page with his picture on it. His name was Ryan McKenna. He was thirteen. The same age as me. His home was in Liverpool, although it didn't give the actual area.

I stared at the picture for a long time, and the boy's eyes stared back at me. It was as if they were calling me. Come and find me, they were saying. I folded the picture and put it in my wallet.

Downstairs Mum and Philip were busy in the office, going through the farm accounts. Lissie was messing about with her phone.

'I'm going for a bike ride,' I called.

'What about lunch?' asked Mum.

'I'll grab a sandwich somewhere.'

'Can I come?' asked Lissie.

'No.' I ignored her disappointed face.

The bike was new, and top of the range. Just two weeks old, a present from Philip for the holidays. A sort of bribe, I supposed, to make me like him.

Liverpool was a five mile bike ride from the farm, and once there it took me a while to find a police station, which I only noticed from the half dozen police cars outside. I parked my bike close to the entrance and went in. A uniformed sergeant was at the enquiry desk. I took out the picture of Ryan and showed it to him.

'I just want to check if you've found this boy yet? I'd like to meet him.'

The sergeant looked at the picture and then at me.

'It's you, isn't it? You playing games with me, son?'

'No, I've only just -'

'Here! Bill, come and see this.'

Another police sergeant joined him, and they both peered at the picture and then at me.

'I'll go and phone his guardian.'

'No, wait! I'm not him, I just -'

'What?'

'I just look like him.'

'Grab him, Bill.'

'Wait! ' I pulled out my wallet. I had my own bank card, another present from Philip. 'See? That's me. And here's my bus travel card. I can prove who I am.' I waited, holding my breath as they pored over the cards.

'OK, but we'll need your address.'

'Why?'

'Because this still seems a bit fishy. Not natural, is it? Two strangers looking so alike?'

I gave them my address. I had to. 'But you will let me know if you find him? This Ryan?'

'We'll see.'

I left, wishing I'd never gone there. What if they contacted Mum? For some reason I didn't want her to know about Ryan.

Ryan

He checked the pockets of his rucksack. All that was left of his £5 note was a single pound coin and a couple of 20p pieces. His money would run out soon.

No more supermarket snacks. Besides, he looked too messy to walk into a supermarket. After nearly a week sleeping rough in the park his clothes were grubby and creased. He'd had a few dips in the lake to clean up, early morning before the park got any visitors, but he was always fearful of getting caught without his clothes.

Food was the immediate problem. He was so hungry, it was hard to think straight. He was tempted to go back to the park cafe. The lady there had been kind, but she would probably insist on calling the police if he turned up a second time.

There was nothing for it but to scavenge through the bins again. It was nearly six o'clock and the park was emptying. The first three bins were filled with nothing but rubbish, but he was lucky at the fourth. A greasy paper bag with a half-eaten burger, still warm, and a waxed carton with about an inch of orange juice still remaining. There was also a copy of the local newspaper. He wrapped the food in it and crept down to the lake. Later, after he'd eaten the remains of the burger, he opened the paper – and was shocked to find the photograph of himself.

Joe must have reported him missing. But why? Ryan had expected he would be pleased to lose him. Unless one of the neighbours, perhaps Melanie's Mum next door, had called the police.

Well, now he'd have to be even more careful. Or go back. He thought of his last day at home, when he had asked Joe for money to buy some food, and reminded him that school would be starting again soon and he needed new this and that.

Joe had exploded then, and lashed out, hitting Ryan across the ear. 'You're not mine,' he'd yelled. 'You're not my responsibility any more.'

No, he couldn't go back. Joe didn't want him, and if the police found him, he'd probably end up in a Home somewhere. Would that be worse than living with Joe, now that his Mum was dead? But where else could he go? And how was he going to survive? He'd run away without any plan, just the desperate urge to get away from Joe and the house that was now so empty. He felt the familiar ache in his throat, the sting of tears in his eyes. But he was too young to live alone, too young to get a job, too young for anything.

'Mum,' he whispered. 'Mum!'

He took out her photograph. She had been so pretty then, her eyes bright, her cheeks bunched in a smile. He didn't want to remember how she looked when she was dying, so thin and pale, her eyes dark and sunken.

'Joe will look after you,' she had whispered on that last day. 'He's promised me.'

But Joe wasn't looking after him. Joe didn't even *look* at him. Joe wanted him gone.

Just then he saw two policemen coming towards him, They were chatting, hadn't noticed him yet. He dodged behind the park's bandstand, ready to run. But for how much longer?

THREE

Simon

I wasn't ready to go home. For want of anything better to do, I cycled to the Pier Head, bought a burger and ate it watching the boats on the river. The Mersey ferry boat was on its way back from Birkenhead, packed with locals and tourists. Alongside me people were taking photographs of it. I took one myself on my phone, thinking it would make a good painting. It was an old boat, probably just grey until some famous artist had decided it would look good painted in brilliant colours, red and orange, blue and yellow, black and white. I thought about exploring the various museums. The Beatles. The Maritime Museum. But I wasn't ready to give up on the boy, although I had no idea where to search next. What would I do, I asked myself, if *I* was running away? Where would I go? I'd probably get on a train to – where? - London? Or maybe the Peak District, or the Highlands up in Scotland, somewhere without too many people. But I had money. Philip was generous. The boy with my face probably had nothing.

No, unless he'd hitched a ride with a truck driver, he could still be somewhere in the city. But where?

I threw the remains of my burger to a gull, who caught it in mid-air. But then -

'Ryan!'

I staggered as two arms clamped themselves around my neck from behind. 'What – who ?'

The girl who had thrown herself at me stepped back. She looked puzzled.

'You look – I don't know – different. Your hair, and – your clothes.' She fingered the collar of my jacket. 'Where d'you get this? Did you steal it?'

'No, of course not!' I was wearing the new Tommy Hilfiger jacket that Philip had bought me. It wasn't much diffferent from my old one but I expect it was quite expensive.

'You – you *are* Ryan, aren't you?'

'No, my name's Simon.'

'Sorry, she said. 'I thought – you're so like. You're sure you're not Ryan? He's run away, and we're all looking for him.' She started to turn away.

'No, wait! This Ryan. He's a friend of yours?'

'Yes, we're mates. We live in the same street, and we go to the same school.'

'I'm looking for him too!' I showed her the newspaper photo. She stared back and forth between the photo and me.

'What d'you want him for? You're not mates, are you? If it's just because you look a bit alike -'

'I really want to meet him. I'd like to get to know him. You must admit, we're more or less identical. Please – don't go. Stay and tell me about him.' I had to keep her here, learn more about the boy. An ice cream van had just pulled up. 'Come on – let me buy you an ice cream and we can sit down and talk.'

She hesitated. 'OK. As long as you're not playing games with me.'

We sat on a bench and she told me how unhappy Ryan had been since his mother died. 'And Mr Geoghegan – he's not Ryan's Dad, he and Ryan's mother are just together, my Mum said. Anyway, he just fell apart. Started drinking, and then he lost his job and started taking it out on Ryan. I don't blame Ryan for doing a runner.'

'Where d'you think he'd go?'

She shrugged. 'Dunno. Maybe Sefton Park? He likes it, and it's big, he could hide there, but I wish he'd told me. I could have helped him.'

'You like him, don't you?' She blushed, and pretended to take an interest in the family of five having their photograph taken beside the statues of the four Beatles.

I checked the time. 'I have to go, but – perhaps we could search for him together? Could we meet up tomorrow?'

She stared at me. 'You're really keen, aren't you?'

'I'm - yes. Wouldn't you be if you found you had a double?'

She nodded. 'I suppose so. But what will you do if we find him? He won't want to go back home.'

I hadn't thought beyond finding him. 'I don't know. I suppose I'd like to help him if I could.'

'And you wouldn't tell the police?'

'No, I promise.'

She stared at me for a long moment and then nodded. 'All right, I'll trust you!'

We fixed a time for the following afternoon.

'What's your name, by the way?'

'Melanie. Melanie Morgan.'

Before she left, she came closer and stared into my face.

'You really are alike, aren't you?' She touched my eyebrows. 'They're the same. And -' She turned my head sideways and giggled. 'You've got the same little twist at the bottom of your noses.'

Back home I found Mum and Philip in the kitchen. She was peeling vegetables for the evening meal and Philip was cutting up a chicken. They were talking about the cow and its new calf.

'Lovely little thing,' said Mum.

I stared at the chicken.

'Is that - ?'

'It's from the freezer, Simon.'

Yes, but where had it been before that? I still hadn't got used to the knowledge that what I was eating might have been running about in the farmyard the day before.

'So, have you had a nice day?' asked Mum.

I nodded. 'I cycled into Liverpool, had a wander around the Pier Head.'

'Go into any of the museums?' asked Philip.

'No, just mooched.'

'You should visit the Walker Art Gallery,' he said.

'Seeing you're interested in art. You could even take your stuff and do some sketching or painting there.'

He was still trying to make friends with me, but it was because of him that I'd been wrenched away from everything I knew, all my friends, and my old school, which I'd enjoyed far more than the snobby boarding school I had to attend now. On the other hand, if I hadn't moved here I would never have known about Ryan , I would never have met Melanie and I would not be planning a search for Ryan, and it would be useful to have an excuse.

I nodded. 'Good idea. I might do that tomorrow.'

'Can I come?' asked Lissie.

She never gave up. 'No,' I said. I heard Mum's sigh. I knew how much she wanted me and Lissie to be friends, but it wasn't going to happen. Apart from being a girl and an irritating, clingy pest, she was part of the trap. The Happy Families trap. Mum and Philip were fooling themselves if they thought that would work.

FOUR

Simon

Melanie was late. I'd been hanging around by the park gates for nearly half an hour. And then I saw her. But not just Melanie. She was leading a straggling procession of other girls, all on bikes, most of which looked as if they'd been rescued off skips.

'They all wanted to come and help,' she said.'

'Where are the boys?'

She shrugged. 'They don't bother with him. They call him Mummy's boy, 'cos she didn't like him going off with them.'

One of the girls was riding an ancient boy's bike. A smaller girl, bundled up in a coat too large for her, was perched on the crossbar.

'Is that allowed?' I asked.

The older girl shrugged 'My Mum said I had to bring her.'

'This is Cheryl,' said Melanie, 'and that's Sandra, and that's Jasmine -' She reeled off another half dozen names.

The girls, all nine of them, stared at me as if I was a ghost.

'That *is* Ryan,' said one. She came closer to me. I could see a smear of chocolate on her chin. 'You're not messing with us, are you? Pretending to be someone else with those fancy clothes and that fancy haircut, and putting on a posh voice?'

'No,' said Melanie. 'He just looks like him – and that's why he wants to meet him.'

I didn't try to take in all the names. I was a bit annoyed. I'd looked forward to just Melanie and me, sneaking round the park like undercover detectives and coming up on Ryan unawares. This way he'd see and hear us coming a mile off.

I couldn't help feeling a little embarrassed too, as we set off. I felt everyone was looking at us, at me, the only boy, on my flashy new bike with this motley gang of girls on their rusty old machines. Only Melanie had a reasonably new bike.

'So, should we split up?' I asked Melanie hopefully.

'I think it's better if we stick together,' she said. 'The park's so big, we could easily miss Ryan, but if he's here and we're making plenty of noise, he's more likely to notice and to come to us.'

'Would he trust you all? I mean, are you sure none of the others would tell on him?'

She glared at me. 'Of course they wouldn't. They all like Ryan, and they're sorry for him. They just want to help.' She turned to the others. 'Right, let's go – make plenty of noise but don't shout Ryan's name. We don't want any policemen noticing us and asking questions.'

After an hour or so the younger ones were beginning to grumble and get bored. We stopped by the lake for a rest, and some of the girls produced bottles of lemonade.

One of them came and sat beside me. 'I'm Jasmine,' she reminded me. 'Ryan and Melanie are my best friends.'

'Oh. Right.'

'I know what you are,' she said. 'You're a Doppelganger! Miss Cuthbert read a story in German class, and that's what you are. You and Ryan really are alike! What would you do if you found him?'

'I don't know.'

'You're not going to tell on him, are you?'

'Of course not! I just know I've got to meet him. And maybe help him if I can.'

She nodded. 'We all want that. He's really nice.' She stared at me intently. 'Are *you* nice?'

I laughed awkwardly. 'I don't know. Probably not.' At least, not recently. Not since Mum had met Philip and my life had changed.

'Ryan's Melanie's boyfriend. She'd be really upset if anything bad happened to him.' She stared at me for a while longer, and then got up and strolled back to join some of the others.

I hadn't thought to bring any food, and I felt a bit mean. I offered to cycle back to the cafe and buy sandwiches. Of course, they all wanted different ones and began to squabble, until Melanie took charge and shut them all up.

At the cafe I was last in a queue of seven, but eventually I got to the counter and gave my order. The woman who was serving stared at me.

'Ryan?' she asked. 'You're looking much better. So, did you go back home?'

I was about to tell her I was someone else, but changed my mind . 'Yes, I'm – everything's OK now.'

'That's good. I was worried about you.'

'Well, as you can see, there was no need.'

She smiled broadly. 'Good. I'm glad I didn't call the police.'

I watched as she packed the sandwiches into a bag. I started to take out my card and then realised it would have my real name on it. Fortunately I had some notes in my wallet. Whatever else I felt about Philip, he was very generous, and my pocket money was now five times more than Mum used to give me. Another bribe, perhaps, but one I didn't mind at all.

'That's quite an order,' she said.

'I'm here with friends.' I hesitated. 'Do you get many runaways in the park?'

'A few, but mostly it's the homeless, people who've lost their jobs, or are on drugs, or just can't cope with life.'

'Where would they sleep? Are there any huts or shelters open?'

'Ha! I can't see the Council allowing that, and I don't suppose any of them have tents. Where did you sleep?'

'Just – amongst some bushes,' I said.

'Well, I'm glad you saw sense and went back home. Bad things can happen to kids on their own.'

'We're having a committee meeting,' said Melanie when I got back with the sandwiches. 'We've searched the whole park now, and there's no sign of Ryan. If he'd wanted to be found, he'd have come out and talked to me – to us. So we think he must have moved on somewhere, and there's no point in staying any longer. Besides, Cheryl's Mum's expecting her back with Sandra.'

'So you're giving up.'

'No! I just don't know what else we can do.' Melanie turned away but not before I could see a glaze of tears in her eyes.

'We bought him a present too,' said Jasmine. 'Because he'd lost his Mum. We all put 50p in, and now he won't get it.'

They were all silent for several minutes, until Melanie crossed her arms and frowned. 'We'll just have to find him then, won't we? But not here, and not now.'

'Go then,' I said. 'I'll stay a bit longer, just in case.'

After they'd gone I collected up all the wrappings. I'd only eaten half a sandwich and I'd bought an extra one. I rewrapped them carefully. I tossed everything else into one of the rubbish bins, then held mine up in the air and turned round slowly, before placing them on top of the other stuff. If Ryan was anywhere near, if he had been watching us, he'd come for the food. Wouldn't he?

I cycled off towards the park gates, but then backtracked, wheeling my bike across the grass, taking care to keep close to cover. When I got within sight of the rubbish bin again, I moved into the shelter of a willow tree and waited. There was no one else around. If he was going to come out of hiding, this would be the time.

I waited an hour, but he didn't take the bait. It got to four o'clock. I would have to go home.

Ryan

Ryan waited until dusk, until the park had emptied.

He had followed his friends as closely as he dared. He had longed to talk to them, and especially to the boy they called Simon. Was he a – whatever Jasmine had called him? He supposed he and the other boy did look alike. It was hard to tell without both of them standing in front of a mirror.

Melanie had been upset, and he'd felt mean, but he couldn't risk coming out of hiding. He knew he could rely on Melanie and the older girls not to tell anyone, but he couldn't rely on the younger ones. It could easily slip out when they were with their Mums and Dads.

The lake lay silent, and there was hardly a rustle from the trees. His eyes took another sweep of his surroundings before he crept out from his latest hiding place and headed for the rubbish bin.

Yes, the boy had left something. A whole sandwich and another half. Ryan snatched them up and darted back into hiding.

FIVE

Simon

Doppelganger, the girl Jasmine had called me. Back home I googled the word. It meant 'An apparition or double of a living person'. It came from the German, mid 19th century, and the odds against having one, an exact double, were something like a trillion to one. Even so, the likeness between myself and Ryan was strong, so strong that Melanie and the other girls – and the woman in the cafe - were taken in by it.

Staring into the mirror I knew I had to find Ryan. Even if we had nothing in common except our faces, even if we disliked each other, I wouldn't be able to rest until I'd found him. I took out the photograph again. Ryan . Aged 13, the same as myself.

On impulse I slipped downstairs and grabbed a pair of scissors from the office. Back in my room I stared into my mirror.

It shouldn't be hard. The sides were already short. I hesitated for only a moment. Then . . .

'Here goes!' I whispered..

It only took me about ten minutes. Grab a clump of hair between two fingers, chop down to the fingers, grab the next clump, chop -

It didn't look *too* bad, I told myself. But Mum would have a fit.

She was calling me down for dinner. She and Philip and Lissie were talking about the calf. Mum was thrilled. It was the first time she'd seen a new-born.

'It's so cute. You should go and see it, Si -' She stopped, and her mouth fell open. 'Oh, my God! What have you done?'

Philip was on his feet. 'What the -?'

I shrugged. 'I wanted a change.'

'It looks like the sea in a Force 8 gale!'

'Well, I'm not planning to be a barber when I grow up!'

'Don't be cheeky. You can't go back to school looking like that! Like – like a young thug!'

'I like it,' I said. 'There were lots of kids at my old school with crew cuts. Anyway, I don't want to go back, do I? I want to go to an ordinary day school here, where I can have mates to knock around with in the evenings and at weekends.' (And with a decent art department, although I didn't say this aloud. They already knew what I wanted to be. Not a farmer. An artist.)

I didn't say either that I wanted to look like Ryan.

'I think it's quite cute,' said Lissie.'You look like a rock star!'

So at least I had one fan, even if it was only my annoying future stepsister.

'More like a ruffian,' said Philip.

'Maybe I can tidy it up,' said Mum, her eyes pleading with him. 'It won't look too bad.'

I didn't stay long downstairs after dinner. Mum was still upset, even after she'd trimmed and levelled my haircut, and Philip wouldn't look at me.

'We'll talk tomorrow,' he said, and turned on the BBC News Channel on television.

Upstairs I took out the photograph of Ryan and held it alongside my reflection in the mirror. Mum had done a good job on my hair, and we could have been the same person.

A trillion to one, I whispered. But there was no mistaking the likeness. We had the same face.

I lay in bed that night, wondering what my next step should be. The sky was already getting lighter when I finally slept.

Ryan

Ryan couldn't sleep either. He'd enjoyed the boy's sandwiches but they were not enough. His stomach was still so empty he felt as if it was stuck to his backbone. He thought about the boy and wondered if he would see him again. If it would be safe to see him again. But the boy couldn't help him. No one could.

The night was cooling. He curled up into a tight ball within a dense clump of bushes, well away from any of the paths and tried to sleep. It was not easy. If the hunger didn't keep him awake, the noises and rustlings of animals and insects disturbed him. The hoot of an owl, the flap of wings, the itchiness after being bitten by insects. In the distance he could hear voices and the bark of a dog. Dogs were the biggest threat. They always wanted to investigate. He held his breath, praying the dog and its owner would stay well away from his hiding place.

It was early morning when he awoke, the sky a pearly grey. The morning chorus of birds had begun. He picked up his belongings and checked his watch. Just after 6.30. He was hungry, and most of all, thirsty. The park's fountain was his main source for water, and at this hour it should be safe to visit it.

He'd become used to a zigzag approach, darting from one group of trees or shrubs to the next, and it wasn't until he was almost upon the fountain that he saw the dark motionless shape, half in, half out of the water. He wanted to turn back, but the figure was motionless, and now he could see it was a man, middle aged, dark suited. Was he ill? Drunk?

He moved closer. The man's eyes were open but unblinking. The man was dead.

Ryan stood there. He didn't know what to do. His urge was to back away, back into hiding, but somebody should call the police. And there was no one else, it was up to him - but he'd have to be well away before they got here. He took out his phone. Hesitated. Who was the man? Would they want to know?

He crept forward. Holding his breath and averting his eyes from the man's face, he slipped his hand into the man's jacket pocket and pulled out a wallet.

There were cards in there, but also – it was packed with money. For long moments Ryan stood there, the wallet open in his hands. He could buy all the food he wanted – for days – weeks. And clothes. And – perhaps even a bike? Secondhand, of course.

His hand was already moving the wallet to his

pocket. It was wrong, he knew it was wrong, but -

'Hey! You there!'

He turned, dropping the wallet. It was the police, two of them, and they were running towards him.

'Stop right there!' one of them yelled.

But Ryan didn't stop. He ran, up the main drive, out the main gates, past a row of shops, their doors barred, their windows still dark, past towering apartment blocks and rows of new-build houses, until he reached the huge old houses on Aigburth Drive that had belonged to the ship owners and the cotton and tobacco merchants of past centuries. The houses still had their walled front gardens, often with dense mature shrubbery. Ryan swerved into one of the gardens and flung himself down behind its high stone wall.

He lay still, his heart thudding, an agonizing pain in his lungs. He had evaded the police, but what now? Where could he go?

At least he still had his rucksack. He never left it behind, not even to steal across to the park's fountain for water. What would he do if someone stole it?

When the thudding in his heart had eased and he could breathe again, he took out his phone.

He should have charged it before he left home. The battery was almost flat, but maybe he could just get a few words with Melanie. Not that she'd be able to help him, and he wouldn't want her to get into trouble, but – just to talk – it would help. He felt so alone. Maybe he'd been a fool to run away. He'd known Joe didn't want him but he'd been shocked when Joe hit him. Now he'd only made things worse for himself. Where could he go? Where could he hide?

Melanie would be having breakfast. His mouth watered as he pictured her tucking into Coco Pops and toast with peanut butter, her favourite breakfast.

'Ryan!' she shrieked when she answered his call.

'Sssh!'

'It's alright, I'm back in my room. Where are you?'

'I'm in one of the front gardens on Aigburth Drive.'

'Which one?'

'I don't know. I'm behind a wall and there are some big trees -'

'They've all got big trees. Can't you creep up and get the house number or name? I'll come out on my bike, and I'll bring you something to eat. It won't be much, Mum hasn't shopped yet, but -'

'You won't tell her? You won't tell *anyone*, will you?'

'Of course I won't. Just get me the number, and give me half an hour. Oh, Ryan, are you OK?'

'I'm OK,' he said, but after the call ended, he was shaking. He didn't think he'd ever cried as much as he had in the past few days. He scrubbed at his eyes and wiped his nose on his sleeve, and took a deep, deep breath.

Melanie was coming. He didn't know what she could do to help him, but just not to be alone would be something.

SIX

Simon

The doorbell rang as we were eating breakfast. Porridge with golden syrup, and two poached eggs on toast. The eggs were freshly laid and collected that morning, and their yolks were a brilliant yellow. I couldn't complain about the food since we came to live at the farm.

Philip frowned. 'Who's that? It's only seven thirty.'

'I'll go,' said Mum.

She was gone several minutes, and then she came back accompanied by two policemen. I recognised one as Bill, the second policeman at the station in Liverpool.

Mum's eyes were wide. 'They want to talk to *you*, Simon.'

Something must have happened to Ryan. The men's faces were grave.

'What's this?' Philip turned to me. 'What have you done?'

'I haven't done anything!'

'A man's body was found in Sefton Park early this morning,' said Bill. 'Your boy was there. Bending over him, helping himself to the man's wallet. He ran away when he saw us.' He nodded to me. 'Fast runner, aren't you, lad? But you'd forgotten that we had your address.'

Ryan. Ryan must have been there. Had he – no, he wouldn't have killed anybody. He was too young. You didn't kill someone when you were only thirteen. I felt sick.

'We'd like to ask Simon here some questions – or should we call him Ryan?'

'Ryan?' I don't understand,' said Mum. 'This is my son, Simon, and he hasn't been outside the door – we've only just finished breakfast! Philip, tell them!'

'She's right,' said Philip. 'Simon's been with us all night and all morning. Sefton Park – that's miles away. How could he be there? And why? And how did you get our address? You've made a mistake!'

The two policemen looked at each other. Bill shrugged.

'Your son came to see us two days ago,' he said. 'He gave this as his address.'

'Simon?' Mum turned to me. 'What is this? What's going on?'

Perhaps it would have been easier if I'd told her at the beginning. I still don't know what stopped me. But now I had no choice.

'I saw his photo in the paper. His name's Ryan. He'd run away from home. And he looked just like me, Mum, except for the hair. I just wanted to meet him. I went to the Police Station first to see if he'd been found. That was two days ago. Then we checked Sefton Park yesterday -'

'We? Who's we?' asked Philip.

'Melanie and her mates. They're Ryan's friends and they're worried about him. His Mum died recently and he's not happy at home.'

'But you don't know him, Simon,' said Mum. 'Just because you look a bit like him -'

'*Exactly* like him. Wait!' I ran upstairs for Ryan's newspaper photo.

'See? That could be me! That's why I wanted to find him.'

'And that's why you chopped your hair off!' said Lissie. 'Wow!'

Philip turned to the policemen. 'If anyone killed your man, it would be this Ryan, not Simon here. How was he killed?'

'We'll know when the postmortem's been done,' said Bill.

'So, at the moment you don't even know how he was murdered?' said Mum.

'*If* he was murdered,' said Philip. 'I suggest you go away until you find out.'

And they left. After that, I had to face an hour of cross-questioning. Both Mum and Simon agreed the likeness was amazing.

Lissie was filled with envy. 'I wish I had someone who looked just like me.'

'Who'd want to look like you?' I snapped, but then felt mean when I saw her stricken face.

'Simon, you don't know what this boy is like, said Mum. 'He might not be very nice.'

'Melanie and her friends all like him. They said everybody in their street liked him. He wouldn't kill anyone.'

But what if I was wrong? How would I know?

Philip and Mum were still arguing when Melanie's call came. He was ordering me to keep away, do nothing, who knew what this boy was capable of, and however much he looked like me, and even if he might be, just might be, a distant cousin or something, he was not our concern. Mum wanted to meet him, see for herself, perhaps even help him somehow, and, based on the fact that he looked like me, she was sure he hadn't murdered anyone. In the end Philip threw up his hands and went out to bring his small herd of cows into the milking parlour.

I took Melanie's call in my bedroom.

'I'm with Ryan,' she said, her voice a whisper. 'He's hiding out in someone's garden, and I've brought him something to eat, but I don't know what to do next. He won't – can't – go back home, but he needs somewhere safer to hide – and he needs some more food – and money – and his clothes are all messy and damp, and – I promised I wouldn't tell anyone, but I don't know how I can help him!'

'My Mum knows about him. And Philip.'

'You told them!'

'No, the police came. They'd seen Ryan running away in the park and they think he killed someone – and they had my address and they thought I was him.'

'He didn't do it! Ryan wouldn't hurt anyone, but

now he's really on the run, and – Simon, we have to find a safe place for him.'

'Look, I'll come out. Tell me where you are.'

I heard her whispering to Ryan, and him whispering back. It felt weird, this boy I was now going to meet and actually talk to. Would even our voices be the same?

'OK.' She was back on the phone. 'We're in a front garden on Aigburth Drive. No. 119. I'll be outside on the pavement, but be careful in case there are any police around. Could you wear a beanie? Maybe sunglasses?'

I laughed. 'I've got a Joker's mask from last year's Halloween? That do?'

'It's not funny, Simon,' she snapped. 'If the police see you they're going to think you're Ryan again, aren't they?'

'Yeah, sorry.'

'And bring more food!' she added.

I knew there'd be questions from Mum and Philip and Lissie, so I didn't tell them where I was going on my bike. When I got to the farm gates I stopped to pull on the beanie, one of the ones Philip wore on early cold mornings out on the fields, and a pair of sunglasses, even though the sun wasn't shining. It was then I heard the thud of footsteps behind me.

'Lissie.' I sighed.

'You know where he is, don't you? You're going to see him!'

'I'm not. I'm just going for a ride. Clear my head.'

'I'll come with you!' she panted. 'Just let me get my

bike.'

'No! This isn't a game. It's serious.'

'But I want to help.'

'Well, you can't. Anyway, you'd just slow me down.'

She glared at me, her lower lip stuck out. 'I'll tell my Dad!'

'If you do, Ryan could end up in prison. Look, I'm wasting time. Go back, and if they ask where I am, just tell them you haven't seen me.' I didn't wait to see what she would do. I pedalled away, as fast as the bike would go.

I had a bag with me, stuffed with bits from the kitchen – left over toast, some fruit, a piece of Mum's chicken and mushroom pie from yesterday, plus a can of pepsi. I wondered what it would be like to be actually starving, and how soon you started losing weight and passing out. I hoped I'd never find out.

I didn't need to search for the house. I saw Melanie from three blocks away, pacing up and down on the pavement, swivelling her head to look behind her, and I thought if I was a policeman I'd regard her as highly suspicious.

As soon as I stopped, she rushed over to me.

'Bring your bike into the garden,' she whispered. 'No one will see you – the house is empty, boarded up. Ryan's waiting for us.'

I felt a sudden rush of adrenalin that took my breath away. I was going to meet my Doppelganger. I wondered if he felt the same excitement. Of course, he had other things on his mind, so probably not. But he stood up as Melanie and I slipped into the garden, and I saw his eyes widen.

We stared at each other for what seemed an hour, with Melanie's eyes switching from Ryan to me, then back to Ryan. I tried to speak but only a whisper came out.

'Hi.'

'Hi,' he whispered back.

'Did you bring more food?' asked Melanie.

I handed the bag over to Ryan. He opened it and began to snatch the food and cram it into his mouth.

'He doesn't usually eat like that,' whispered Melanie. 'He's got quite good manners.'

We watched for perhaps five minutes until all the food was gone. Ryan folded up the bag and handed it back to me. 'Thank you,' he said, and then he clapped his hand to his mouth, turned away to some bushes and threw up all that he'd eaten.

'Well, that was a waste,' Melanie said sadly.

'I can get more.'

'But the main thing is to find a safe place for Ryan,' she said.

'I didn't kill anyone,' said Ryan. 'The man was dead when I found him. Honestly.'

His voice was like mine, I thought, although his accent was a little different.

'We know,' said Melanie. 'But until the police find who killed him, you're not safe.' She turned to me. 'Got any ideas, Simon?'

I turned to Ryan. 'There's lots of room at the farm –

and I think my Mum would like to help you,' I said. 'But not Philip, Mum's partner. At least, not while the police think you might be a murderer -'

'But I'm not! I swear -'

'We know,' said Melanie quickly. She pulled Ryan into a hug and patted his back, as if he was a small child. 'It'll be alright, you'll see.'

Meanwhile I was thinking.

'I've got an idea. There's an old cottage on the southern edge of the farm. It's got a separate little lane leading to it from the road, hardly a car's width. Nobody's lived there for at least twenty years, Philip said. One day he plans to do it up, but right now it's a mess, the roof leaks, there's no running water, no anything, but you could hide out there, Ryan – at least until the police find their murderer and you're off the hook.'

They were both looking at me as if I was Jesus. It felt good.

'I could bring you food and stuff, and Melanie, you could go straight there on your bike without coming through the farm.'

'But what about this Philip?' asked Ryan. 'What if he decided to visit?'

'He never has, since Mum and I have been there, but if he did – well, Mum might persuade him to keep quiet. But if the police still think you killed this man -'

'I didn't!'

'OK, OK. Well, at least we might have a day or so before we hear from them again. And if they're still coming after you, I could help you get away. I could give you some money, and clothes - and my bike. It's a racer and it's fast -'

'You'd do all that for me? You'd even lend me your bike? Why?'

I shrugged. 'I never asked for it. Anyway, I just want to help – and keep in touch. I feel we're connected. Don't you?'

He shrugged. 'Maybe.'

Melanie dug into the bag she carried over her shoulder and pulled out a mirror. 'Here,' she said. 'Look at yourselves. You must be connected in some way.'

Almost reluctantly, Ryan put his head next to mine and we stared into the small mirror.

'We must be,' he said at last. 'I can't see any differences.'

SEVEN

Simon

I gave Ryan my beanie and my sunglasses. And then I gave him my bike.

'It's a loan at the moment,' I told him. 'But if you ever need it to escape, I promise you can have it.'

His eyes widened. His fingers ran over the handlebars as if he was scared the bike might vanish. His face screwed up as if he was fighting back tears.

'Thanks,' he muttered.

I gave Melanie directions to the farm, and then to the cottage. 'Make sure you keep out of sight and keep quiet. You don't want the animals taking an interest.'

'What animals?' she asked. She looked a bit apprehensive.

'Cows. Sheep. They're always curious and if they hang about near the cottage, Philip might come and find you.' I glanced at my watch. 'I have to go. The cottage is boarded up at the front but there's a back door, although you'll probably have to heave it open. I'll meet you there in about an hour and a half.'

Ryan

Ryan hadn't had a bike of his own since he and

themselves against the tiny window.

'We'll ask Simon if he can lend you a sleeping bag and a pillow.' Melanie clicked a switch by the door. 'No electricity. Never mind, I expect he can let you have a torch – and next time I come I'll bring you some nice bits and pieces,' she added, seeing his downcast face.

She came closer and wrapped her arms around him. 'Be grateful, Ryan. Things could be worse – and I'm sure everything will sort itself out soon.'

Ryan didn't believe her but he smiled and nodded.

Simon

I was quite pleased that the taxi driver refused to take me down the lane to the cottage. It meant that others would be discouraged too, although it also meant that I would have to carry two heavy bags of shopping the rest of the way. The taxi fare and the shopping had taken all the money I had in my wallet but I didn't care.

'It's OK, it's me,' I said as I opened the back door of the cottage and dumped the bags inside.

'I brought some food. And some loo rolls and stuff. There's no bathroom, you'll have to wash in the sink with bottled water, but there's a privy in that little shed down the garden.'

'Thanks,' Ryan muttered. He was still looking pretty sorry for himself and I began to feel a little annoyed. I'd put myself out for him and spent all my pocket money. He could be a little more grateful. But then I imagined how I would feel in his position, Mum dead, nowhere to live, starving, the police hunting him.

'Don't worry, I promise I'll help.'

'Me too,' said Melanie. 'I'll come back tomorrow morning.'

'I'll have to take my bike back now,' I said, 'but I'll be round again soon with more stuff. Why don't you sort yourself something to eat while I'm gone – seeing you threw up all the last lot!'

Back at the house I went to find Mum. She was in her and Philip's bedroom, putting on makeup. Her eyes were swollen.

'What's up?'

'I don't know. It was just such a shock, seeing that photo.' She put down the cream she'd been stroking around her eyes. 'I keep thinking, it could have been you. I know you're not really happy here, Simon. I thought you'd love it, and I know Philip's trying his best.'

'It's alright. *I'm* not going to run away, Mum, I promise.'

'Give us a hug then!'

And I did.

Later, after dinner, I searched for my old sleeping bag, grabbed a couple of towels and some soap, a pillow, a tracksuit, a sweater and a torch, and shoved the lot into a couple of bin bags. Was there anything else? I hesitated. It was still only seven o'clock. It was going to be a long lonely night for him.

I didn't really want to part with it but at the last minute I added my MP3 player. It was charged up, and it was something to keep him company.

When everything was ready I checked the house. Mum and Philip were in the sitting room, watching The One Show.

'Joining us?' asked Philip.

'No, thanks. Not my thing. I'm going to do some sketching in my room and then have an early night. Where's Lissie?'

'Probably in her room,' said Mum. 'Why don't you ask her to pose for you? I bet she'd love you to do a portrait.'

I shrugged. 'Maybe one day. Not tonight.'

Upstairs I listened at her door. She was playing her favourite programme. Dating, make up, fashions, she never tired of it.

I gathered up my stuff and crept down to the back door.

The light was already fading when I reached the cottage. Inside, the air was cool. Ryan was sitting cross-legged in a corner of the stone floor, my jacket beneath him, everything else hugged closely around his body. He was shivering. Tomorrow, I decided, I would bring him a flask of hot cocoa.

'Hello,' I whispered. 'Have you eaten?'

He nodded.

'Want to see what I've brought?' I started to pull stuff out of the bin bag, but he didn't seem interested. I think he was seriously depressed. His face was grubby, and even in the gloom I could see tear streaks glistening on his cheeks. I spread out the sleeping bag. 'It's a good one, should keep you warm tonight – and here's a torch, just don't point it at the windows.' I turned it on and pointed it at my own face. 'See?'

It was only when I took out my MP3 player that he showed any interest.

'Why are you doing all this? You don't know anything about me. Just because we look alike, it doesn't make us mates, does it?'

I was hurt.

'If I didn't look like you, you wouldn't bother, would you?'

Would I? Was this connection I felt just me being conceited? Because he looked like me, he must be special? Perhaps I should just let him go. He could take all the stuff I'd bought – but not my bike – and disappear. Why should I care?

Just then I heard the door creak open and I saw Ryan's eyes widen as he looked over my shoulder.

'Yoohoo! It's me!'

Oh my God, it was Lissie. I leapt up and shut the door behind her. 'What are you doing here?' I hissed.

'I followed you. You've been so sneaky. I saw you creeping out with those bags. I knew something was going on, and if you don't let me stay, I'll tell my Dad, and your Mum!' She stared at Ryan. 'Oh, wow!'

For at least fifteen seconds she was silent, her eyes switching between us. Then, 'Wow! She whispered again. 'You really are like two peas, aren't you? You're even wearing the same clothes. That sweater's Simon's, isn't it? I bet my Dad wouldn't be able to tell you apart! My Dad and Simon's Mum are getting married in October,' she chatted on. 'Simon and me are going to be stepbrother and stepsister. You got any sisters, Ryan?'

Ryan shook his head. He was looking nervous again. 'She won't tell, will she?' he asked me.

'Of course I won't!' Lissie was indignant. But then she smiled at me. 'As long as I can come with you and help look after Ryan.'

'This isn't a game, Lissie. Ryan could go to jail if

he's found!'

'I know, and I shan't really tell on you – as long as you let me help.'

'Should I kill you right now, or when you're in bed and asleep? You're too young to help – and too stupid. You're bound to let something slip to Mum or Philip.'

'I won't! I promise!' She turned to Ryan. 'I can bring you more stuff – and I can warn Simon if my Dad's anywhere near. I can be your lookout!'

'Stop it!' Ryan was on his feet, glaring at us both. 'Just go away, both of you. All I want to do is sleep.' He turned his back on us and began to unroll the sleeping bag.

'This is exciting, isn't it?' Lissie whispered as we crept back to the house. I refused to answer. I probably would never speak to her again.

EIGHT

Simon

I never oversleep, but the next day I slept through breakfast and all the usual morning sounds, the mooing of the cows as Philip brought them into the milking shed, the pounding of the washing machine and Mum's humming as she came up the stairs.

She opened my bedroom door. She was carrying a mug of coffee.

'Good morning, sleepyhead. What were *you* doing last night?'

'What? Where – What time is it?' I shot out of bed, catching my foot in the sheet .

'Careful. Watch the – oh, too late.' Coffee pooled on the rug beside my bed. 'What's the hurry?'

'Oh, nothing,' I said. Melanie might already be at the cottage, and Lissie – what was she doing? 'I just don't like oversleeping.'

Mum looked at me, disbelief in her eyes. 'Hmmm.' She rolled up the steaming rug. 'I'll take this down and scrub it. I expect you'll still want breakfast?'

'Not hungry,' I said, but then I remembered I'd planned to take some more food down to Ryan. 'Well, maybe just some toast.'

'You'll have to make it yourself. Half the morning gone, I've things to do.'

That suited me. I could sneak some more stuff from the fridge and the pantry. 'Where's Lissie?' I asked. Casually.

'Oh, somewhere around.'

Somewhere around the cottage, I thought.

I was right. After I'd gulped down some toast and shoved some bread, a banana and a couple of apples into a bag, I rushed down to the cottage. Melanie was already there. I saw her bike, fairly well hidden behind one of the bushes. I could hear voices from inside the cottage. Ryan and Melanie. And Lissie. I really would have to kill her.

'Oh, hi, Simon,' said Melanie as I pushed open the door. 'Your sister's been telling us all about the baby calf and how embarrassed you were!'

I glared at Lissie. She glared back at me.

'She's not my sister!' I turned my back on her and took my bag of food over to Ryan. He was looking better this morning, almost cheerful. I guess that was because Melanie was there. Lissie surveyed the few bits I laid out for him. She sniffed.

'*I* brought him apple pie and chocolate biscuits!'

I ignored her.

'So – What's been happening?' I asked Melanie. 'Anything from the police?'

'They came round to see Mr. Geoghegan, but I don't know what was said.'

'They probably still think I killed that man,' said Ryan. 'But I didn't.'

'We know that,' said Melanie. 'I'll ask my Mum and Dad if they've heard anything.'

'There'll be a postmortem.' I said.

'How long does that take?'

'Dunno, but I expect they'll tell Mum and Philip when it's done – seeing as they came here to accuse *me*!'

Ryan was beginning to look gloomy again. 'Maybe I should go, find somewhere else to hide?'

'No, you're safe here. Philip doesn't have any reason to come to the cottage. As long as we're quiet – and as long as we stop playing tea parties!' I glared at Lissie. I'd noticed the tray and the paper napkins, knife, fork and spoon in a serviette ring.

The next morning Melanie was back, but this time she had brought Jasmine. I was a bit put out, that she hadn't asked my permission. Lissie, who'd tagged along, noticed.

'It's not your cottage, you know. It belongs to my Dad.'

'I know, but it was my idea for Ryan to stay here, and I'm the one who'll be in trouble if he finds out.'

Melanie and Jasmine spent ages hugging Ryan and reassuring him that everything was going to turn out well. I couldn't help noticing how much more cheerful he was with them around.

They had brought him presents. A knitted balaclava and a scarf from Melanie ('In case it's cold at night'), a cushion from Jasmine ('To keep you comfy').

That was just the start. Over the next three days they brought more stuff, and that encouraged Lissie to swipe stuff from the house – cups and saucers (*saucers – anyone would think this was a hotel!*), copies of the latest comics, a vase filled with flowers she'd picked on the way.

The girls were having fun, the cottage was becoming a play house, and it was getting noisy. Ryan was enjoying it all, I could tell. I was the only one who was feeling grumpy.

I couldn't really complain to Melanie and Jasmine, except to suggest they should keep the noise down, but I could have a go at Lissie.

'Time to go,' I told her. 'We don't want Philip and my Mum searching for us. And Lissie, will you stop bringing silly stuff to the cottage. We're not kids playing Mums and Dads. What would *your* Dad say if he came to the cottage and saw it filled with tea sets and ornaments and frilly bits?'

She didn't reply, but as we were making our way back across the fields she turned and glared at me.

'I'm not stupid, you know. You treat me like an irritating kid of six. You don't treat Melanie or Jasmine like that and they're only two years older than me, they told me so. I'm just trying to make things more cheerful for Ryan. I like him. He's nice.'

She looked up at me. 'Nicer than you!'

We walked in silence after that.

Lissie and Melanie, sometimes with Jasmine, sometimes without, came regularly now, and Ryan was happier. We were all having fun, I suppose, but the noise level was rising by the day. I was worried that Philip might hear us.

'It's got to stop,' I said. 'I could hear you from two fields away!'

'It'll have to stop soon,' said Melanie. 'Back to school in three weeks and four days.'

'Except for me,' said Ryan.

'You have to give yourself up,' she said.

'They'll make me go back to Joe – or put me in a Home.'

'It mightn't be that bad,' said Melanie. 'You might get nice foster parents.'

'No!'

'Well, you can stay here for now,' I said, 'but *I'll* be away soon – mine's a boarding school.'

'Oh, wow!' said Melanie. 'What's it like?'

'Horrible.'

'Do you get beaten?' asked Jasmine.

'All the time!' I didn't, but it was fun to see her horrified face.

So Lissie told them about her boarding school, which she seemed to enjoy, and the girls were even more interested.

I looked at my watch. 'Time to go,' I said.

After Melanie and Jasmine had gone, Lissie and I walked back across the fields. I kept a lookout for Philip. Every day I had to check on his whereabouts, and if there was any risk of his coming close to the cottage I'd have to phone Ryan and get him to hide in the upstairs room. I had charged his phone, so at least we were able to communicate now.

We found Philip checking his sheep. 'Got some foot rot here. Want to help?' he called.

'OK,' said Lissie cheerfully, and hopped over the fence to join him.

'Simon?'

I shuddered. 'No thanks.' I walked on. I was never going to turn into a farmer, and Philip would have to accept that.

I found Mum in the dairy. One of the neighbouring

farmers' wives was teaching her how to make cheese, and she seemed to be enjoying it. I thought back to the days when we had lived in London and she had worked in an office, making lots of phone calls to sell TV advertising to businesses. She had been good at it. Didn't she miss it? Didn't she miss our life, the park across the road, the shops and cafes and the leisure centre just around the corner? Her friends? It was like Philip had cast a spell on her, and there was hardly time for anything or anyone else. Not even me.

'Don't come in!' she called. 'You're not hygienic!'

She and her friend were all kitted out. White caps on their heads, masks, huge white aprons, even bags on their feet like police wear when they're investigating a murder.

I turned away. There was nothing for me here.

Philip and Lissie didn't come back until lunchtime. They were tired and dirty, but cheerful. Mum was back in the kitchen by then, heating up a big pan of soup and baking rolls to eat with it.

'All done,' said Philip. 'Thanks for your help, Lissie.'

I guessed he was saying that for my benefit, to make me feel guilty. I didn't care. But I was feeling pretty gloomy.

I thought about Melanie's visits with Jasmine to see Ryan. The three of them didn't need anyone else, did they? Certainly not me, even though I'd helped Ryan more than anyone. Why didn't he like me? But when I thought about it, did I really like him? I wanted to, I definitely wanted us to be mates, but I hadn't really found any reason for that, except that he was my double. Was he right? Was it just conceit? Did I want him just as my own personal mirror?

'Don't you like the soup, Simon?' asked Mum.

I gulped a mouthful. 'Yes, great. Just not very hungry.'

'You didn't have much for breakfast. You OK?'

I nodded. 'Just tired. I might go and do some sketching.' I could feel her eyes on me as I took my bowl over to the sink and tipped out the soup I hadn't eaten. Ryan would have liked it, I thought, but I couldn't go back to the cottage, not yet.

I hadn't been in my room long before there was a knock on the door. It opened, and there stood Lissie.

'Mum said you might sketch me sometime.'

Mum. Lissie had called my mother Mum right from the start. Did they all expect me to call Simon Dad? Well, that was never going to happen.

'Not now, Lissie. I'm not in the mood.'

'You never are.' She came and sat on the end of my bed. 'I wish we could be friends. It's silly, both of us being miserable.'

'*You've* no reason to be miserable,' I said.

Her face crumpled up. 'It's my birthday in a few weeks.'

'Really? I'd forgotten.' I supposed I'd have to buy her something, but I'd have to get a sub from Philip, or perhaps it would be better to ask Mum. Philip would want to know what I'd spent all last week's pocket money on.

'Are Mum and Philip having a party for you?'

She shrugged.

'So, what's making you miserable? You'll be

twelve, nearly a teenager.'

She said nothing for a while, and then: 'Just wondering if my Mum will remember. She didn't last year.'

I'd forgotten about Lissie's Mum. She was never mentioned by anyone. What had happened to her? Where was she? No one ever said.

'She lives in America. She got married again and she's got a new baby. I haven't heard from her since last Christmas.'

'Sorry,' I said.

We were both silent for a while, and then she scrubbed at her eyes and sat upright. 'What about you? Does your Dad ever call or write to you?'

'I don't know my Dad, and he doesn't know me. He probably doesn't even know I exist. He and Mum were both still at school. Mum left early when she got pregnant, and I don't think she ever saw him again.'

It didn't hurt at all that my father hadn't wanted to know me. Would it have been different if, like Lissie's Mum, he had been close and had then abandoned me?

Lissie was a pain, always tagging along after me, but still . . .

I sighed and got up off the bed. I opened a drawer in the chest by the window and pulled out my biggest sketching pad and a stick of charcoal.

'OK, where do you want to sit?'

Ryan

Ryan tucked himself back inside Simon's sleeping bag. Although it was summer, the light and warmth of the sun barely penetrated the small, dirt-crusted windows of the cottage and the room was chilly. For the first time since he had run away his stomach was full and Melanie had left enough food for him to eat later, but now she was gone and the rest of the day stretched before him, boring and miserable.

He poked around in the bag of food, picked out an apple and took a bite, then set it down. Maybe he should ask Simon to bring him a book, something exciting, but it was too dark in the cottage to read.

He wished he could turn back time. Bring his Mum back. His whole world had been built around her, Joe's world too. Now she was gone and everything had fallen apart. But things hadn't been good for years now, not since Mum had met Joe and the three of them had left Cornwall.

She hadn't liked Liverpool. She never wanted to go out, didn't want Ryan to go out, would have kept him home from school if it was allowed. And then she became ill and he had watched her shrink into herself, like one of the hermit crabs on the Cornish beaches. And then she had died.

He wondered what Joe was doing right now. Probably in one of the local pubs. He always had money to spend on booze, even though he'd lost his job. Once again Ryan wondered if he he had done the right thing by running away. Perhaps it was Mum's death that had made Joe so angry. Perhaps he had blamed Ryan and that's why he started hitting him. Perhaps he was already regretting it, as Ryan was beginning to regret running away. At least in the street Ryan had had his mates. But it was too late now to change his mind.

He squinted at his watch. Only two o'clock. He

couldn't just sit here for the rest of the day. At least in the park he had been able to move about, feel the warmth of the sun, watch other people.

Simon had said that Philip never came near the cottage. Would it be such a big risk to creep outside? Take a little walk? Enjoy the summer afternoon?

He rolled down the sleeping bag, stuffed his bits and pieces into his rucksack, gathered up the remains of the food, and carried everything up to the bedroom.

And then he opened the cottage's door.

NINE

Ryan

The sun was warm on his head, the air smelled of hay and blossom, with a distant whiff of manure, and he could hear the harsh squawk of crows in the trees that bordered the lane. He took a few cautious steps, ears pricked, eyes alert for any signs of movement around him. Nothing. Even the crows had shut up.

More confident now, he stepped out across an unmown field. In the farthest corner he could see a stile, bordered by hedging. He would take a peep when he reached it, just to see what lay beyond, and then he would turn back. No point in taking unnecessary risks. He thought about Simon as he ploughed through the tall grass. How lucky he was. All this, and yet he didn't look happy. Ryan would swap with him in a second.

He slowed as he neared the stile and listened to the silence. But then the silence was broken by a faint cry.

'Help!' someone was calling. 'Help!'

It was a man's voice. Philip, Lissie's Dad? 'Help me,' the man called again.

I don't have to do anything, Ryan thought. Someone will come. Someone from the house. He waited. No one came.

'Help!' The man's voice was more of a groan now. And still no one came.

Ryan climbed over the stile. He could see the man now, curled on the grass on the far side of the field. Ryan started towards him.

Simon

It hadn't taken me long. An hour, maybe, and I was quite pleased with it.

'Can I see?' asked Lissie. She'd been pestering me for the whole hour. Twice I'd threatened to stop and rub it out if she didn't shut up, but I didn't really mean it. Actually, I thought it was one of the best portraits I'd done, and I'd been quite surprised to see things in her face that I'd never noticed before. *Not* surprising really, seeing as I'd done my best to ignore her over the past six months.

I turned my board towards her and she stared at the drawing for ages. And then she ran out of the room, slamming the door behind her. I guessed she hated it. I grabbed a cloth and was about to rub it out but then I hesitated. I thought it was an honest representation, and even if she didn't want it, I might as well show it to Philip, so I carried it downstairs.

I found Lissie wrapped in my Mum's arms.

Mum turned to me, nodding and smiling.

'She absolutely loves it, Simon. Thank you!' Lissie burrowed her head under Mum's arm but I could see she was nodding too.

'And Philip will love it too. He'll probably want to get it framed.'

'Where is Philip?'

'He's out there repairing some fences. He's been gone quite a while.'

I hoped he wasn't working anywhere near the cottage. Perhaps I'd go down there later, just to check. But all that creative work had made me hungry. 'Any cookies?' I asked.

'In the tin.'

I grabbed two, and then wrapped a couple more in a piece of kitchen roll and slipped them into my pocket. Later I would grab some more food and sneak out to feed Ryan. Maybe I would even let Lissie come, provided she could learn to keep her mouth shut. I didn't want to admit it, but she did seem better than me at cheering him up.

Ryan

The man was half kneeling, half lying against the fence. Ryan could see blood across his right cheek and down his right arm.

'Simon!' the man cried. 'Help me!'

Simon! The man – Philip – thought he was Simon. Ryan took a step backwards, prepared to run, to get back to the cottage, grab his things and move on. Where? Anywhere! But then the man groaned. He was in pain.

'You have to cut this wire off me. I dropped the cutters, I can't reach them. Hurry – I'm losing the circulation to my arm!'

The wire, freed at one end from the fence, had wrapped itself so tightly around Philip's arm and upper body that Ryan had difficulty getting the cutters underneath it, and Philip gasped.

'Sorry!' said Ryan.

'Whiplash,' said Philip. 'It's high tensile wire. I should have known better, wasn't thinking straight.'

It seemed to take an age but at last Philip was free of the wire, and Ryan helped him to his feet.

'Feel a bit groggy,' said Philip. 'Can you help me back to the house?'

Ryan nodded. He mustn't talk. He and Simon had different accents. He put his shoulder under Philip's left arm, helping to take his weight. Which way was the house? He didn't know. He waited for Philip to start moving.

They had crossed two more fields before Philip spoke again. 'Thank you for your help, Simon. I appreciate it.' He smiled down at Ryan. 'I'm not the enemy, you know. Just tell me what you want, and how we can make things better, and I'll do what I can. It would make your mother so happy if we could be friends.'

'OK,' said Ryan. He couldn't risk any more words, but he liked the man. It was hard to understand why Simon was so against him.

When the farmhouse came into view he gasped. Outside, on the drive, a police car was parked.

'Ah! Must be news about the man in the park,' said Philip. 'Let's see if they've let you off the hook, shall we?' He staggered slightly as the boy pulled away.

'Simon? Simon!' he called, but Ryan was already a field away and rapidly disappearing from sight.

Simon

Mum was insisting we wait for Philip. She had called his phone but there was no reply. The policeman – Bill again – was shifting uncomfortably and looking at his watch.

'I have to be somewhere,' he said.

'We wait for Philip,' said Mum. 'He has to be here when you tell us – whatever you want to tell us.' And at that moment the door opened and there stood Philip. His shirt was torn and there was dried blood on his face and all down one arm.

'Dad!' Lissie shrieked. 'You're bleeding!'

'Oh my God!' said Mum. 'What happened?'

'I'm alright. Just had a battle with one of the fences. Simon helped.' And then he saw me. 'Simon? How did you – Who - ?' He glanced round, bewildered.

'Simon's been here all the time,' said Mum.

'Then who - ? And I could see the realisation dawning on his face. 'The boy – Ryan - ?'

'He's not here,' I said quickly.

Bill came forward. 'It wouldn't matter if he was. He's not in trouble. None of you are.'

'Does that mean you've found the murderer?' asked Mum.

'There was no murder. The man died of natural causes,' said Bill.

'When did you know?'

'The postmortem was done the same day. It showed he died from heart failure, following an excess of alcohol and drugs.'

Philip sat down. 'So both Simon and the boy Ryan are off the hook? And you didn't think to inform us right away? You let us carry on worrying until now?'

Bill shuffled. 'I'm sorry. There's been a lot of activity in the city centre. Gang battles. It's been all hands to the deck. Sorry!'

'So does this mean Ryan can come and go wherever

he wants?' I asked.

'If and when we find him, he'll be returned home.'

'Whether he wants to be there or not?'

'Mr Geoghegan isn't pressing for his return, but the boy's only thirteen. He's at risk. If he doesn't go home we still need to find him somewhere to live. Foster parents, or a group home.'

'I'd like to know what happens to him. My son – he's very interested in the boy and you can see why. I don't suppose you could let us have a phone number for his guardian?' Mum smiled at Bill, and when Mum smiles at someone it's very hard for them to say No, so the next moment she'd fetched a notepad and Bill was writing down a number.

I was thinking. I had to find Ryan and tell him he was safe. I wished the policeman would leave – now! As if he heard me, he stood up.

'I'll see you out,' said Mum.

'Where is he?' I asked Philip after Bill had gone.

'I don't know. I turned around and he'd disappeared. He must have run when he saw the police car.'

'He's been staying in the cottage,' I told him. 'He may still be there. I have to go and find him.' I made for the door, but stopped before I reached it.

'If he's still there – Can he stay with us? At least for a while?'

I couldn't wait for an answer. I just took off, hoping I'd reach Ryan before he disappeared.

The cottage was empty. Somehow I knew, even before I opened the door and called his name. All his belongings had gone. There was no evidence of his having been there, except for a few apple cores and an empty cola bottle. I went upstairs. The room was empty. Even the sleeping bag I'd given him was gone.

But he couldn't have got very far on foot, and he could have gone in only one direction – back to the main road. I wished I'd brought my bike. I would have been able to catch him up easily. Instead, I raced downstairs, out of the cottage and along the lane. At the junction I looked both ways. I had to make a choice. I decided he would choose to move on, rather than backtrack to the city. Of course, he could have thumbed a lift, and then I had no hope of finding him.

I hesitated for a few more seconds. And then I began to jog along the road, pausing at every possible hiding place.

It didn't take long. I found him crouching in a ditch alongside the entrance to a stables and riding school. I leaped into the ditch and crouched beside him.

He didn't look at me, just sat there, picking at the skin on his hands. A police car, siren shrilling, came past and he shrank down in the ditch.

'Ryan, it's OK. You're safe! The police came to tell us the man died of natural causes. You didn't kill him. Nobody did.'

He stared at me then and I stared back, and I wanted to hug him but that would have been weird.

'But – I still can't go back home. There's nowhere for me.' He turned away from me, scrubbing at his eyes.

'I think there is, Ryan. I'm pretty sure my Mum and Philip will let you stay with us. I'm pretty sure I – and Lissie, too – can persuade them! Come back. Please!'

I wondered what Mum would make of him. He must have been crying. His eyes were red-rimmed and the skin around his lips was dry and peeling, and he looked pretty grubby. Mum would want to put him straight into the shower, but after that I was sure she'd want to take care of him. And Philip? Ryan had rescued him, and Philip was grateful. He wouldn't send him away. Would he?

TEN

Simon

'Everything's going to be OK from now on,' I had told Ryan. But was it? Mum was so soft hearted, she would want to help, but could she persuade Philip? My fingers were crossed as we went into the house.

Lissie was hovering in the hall. She rushed forward and flung her arms around Ryan. Her nose wrinkled a bit at the smell but she didn't let go.

'You can stay! They said yes!'

And then Mum was there.

'Oh my God! Oh my God!' she whispered. Her eyes switched from Ryan to me, and back again. 'It's – it's unbelievable. Philip, come and see!'

Philip had changed his clothes. His arm was bandaged and a large plaster covered the cuts to his face.

'Ryan, I have to thank you -' he started to say, and then he fell silent.

We were all silent, even Lissie, until Mum stretched out a hand and touched Ryan's cheek. 'Would you like a nice hot shower, Ryan?' she asked gently. 'And then perhaps something to eat?'

He nodded.

'Show him, Simon,' she said to me, 'and find some

clothes for him.'

I sorted out some stuff for him, pants, jeans and a grey sweatshirt, and showed him the bathroom.

'What size shoes do you take?' I asked, and wasn't surprised when he said Size 7, the same as me.

After he'd showered and dressed, I said, 'Come and look in the mirror.' We stood there, side by side, dressed in my clothes, same greeny grey eyes, same light brown hair cropped short, same height, same everything.

'No one could tell us apart,' I whispered.

Before we went downstairs I phoned Melanie and told her what had happened. 'The police came to tell us the man in the park died of natural causes, so Ryan's safe.'

She wanted to speak to Ryan but Mum was calling us.

When we came down, Mum had made a big pot of tea and set out plates of cookies and cake, but for Ryan she had also heated up a large bowl of soup. Her eyes widened when she saw him again, all cleaned up and wearing my clothes but she didn't say anything, and Ryan had eyes for nothing but the food. He started to breathe quickly. She put her hand gently on his head. 'It's alright. Just eat. We can talk another time.'

I suppose the food me and the girls had brought him was more snacky than solid, and when we sat down I could see it was an effort for him to drink the soup slowly. Had he been alone, I think he would have lifted the bowl to his mouth and gulped it down.

None of us said much until he had finished the soup, plus three cookies and two thick slices of cake, and sat back in his chair with a sigh. His eyes were closing.

'I think you need to sleep now,' said Mum. 'Sleep for as long as you need to. We'll talk when you wake up. And don't worry,' she said, touching his shoulder. 'You're safe now.'

Ryan

Simon's mother had made up a bed for him in what she called the guest bedroom. She had left a mug of hot milk on the bedside table He drank it and then stretched his toes down beneath the duvet, enjoying the cool smoothness and the scent of something flowery. Although he ached with tiredness, he couldn't sleep. He turned on and off the small television set on the chest of drawers opposite the bed and he played a few games on the iPad that Simon had lent him, but soon lost interest.

He lay back in bed and stared at the ceiling, at the two huge beams that crossed it. The house was old, really old, and it creaked and sighed. He wondered if there were any ghosts, the spirits of people who'd lived here in the past. And then there were the sounds from outside. Not the sounds he'd been used to at home, the rumble of traffic and the sounding of horns, the beat of music through the thin walls of the houses either side, the shouts and laughter from the street after the pubs closed. Here there was just the sighing of the wind in the eaves, the rustling of trees outside the window, the hoot of an owl.

He liked it, all of it. He liked Lissie, he liked Simon, although it was really strange, really creepy, to look and talk to someone exactly like himself. Simon's mother was really nice, kind and soft, and she looked at him as if she'd like to hug and kiss him, like his own Mum used to – but he was not going to think about Mum. He took a deep breath and held it, squeezed his eyes tight shut. Mum was gone and was never coming back.

He thought about Philip. Simon's stepfather. No, not stepfather, more like Joe, he supposed, a sort of guardian. He sensed that Philip and Simon were not really used to each other yet, but at least Philip was unlikely to get drunk or to raise his hand to Simon.

Before he closed his eyes, Ryan resolved that tomorrow he would do everything he could to make all the family like him, and then they might agree to let him live with them. Forever.

Simon

My phone woke me at six thirty.

'What? Who - ? I squinted at the screen.

'It's me, Melanie! What's happening?'

'Do you know what time it is?'

'Never mind that. How's Ryan? Is he OK?'

'He's fine. He's here, in the spare room - and still asleep, I suppose, like I should be,' I muttered, although I felt a bit guilty. I should have called her.

"So what happens next? Will he have to go back home?'

'Maybe not. Mum really likes him. I think she'd like to keep him here, but I'm not sure yet about Philip. Not as something permanent.'

'Well, Mr Geoghegan doesn't want him back, he didn't even inform the police, my Dad did that.'

'Really? Well, if you're sure, I'll talk to Mum and

Philip again.'

'Do that!' Melanie ordered, and ended the call.

Ryan didn't come down to breakfast. The morning stretched on, with Mum peeping into his room now and then and reporting back.

'He's still asleep. Poor boy, he must have been exhausted.'

I hung around in the kitchen, feeling as if everything was on hold. Outside, huge dark clouds hung heavy in the sky. Rain was forecast, so I didn't want to go out on my bike. In any case, I wanted to be here when Ryan woke up.

Philip was out. The farm kept him busy all day. It was what they called a mixed farm. Crops – corn and barley and stuff, cows, sheep, chickens, even a couple of goats. Mum had thrown herself into it all. Her latest cheese was going to be made from the goats' milk. I knew she wanted me to get involved in the farm too – I saw the disappointment in her eyes every day – but I wasn't going to give in.

Ryan finally appeared as she was setting the table for lunch. He was washed and dressed, in more of my clothes, and I saw Mum's eyes widen.

'Oh, my goodness, I'll have to get used to this! You and Simon – so alike!' She smiled at him. 'I guess you'll be hungry again?' Ryan nodded, speechless.

She sent Lissie to fetch Philip, and we all sat down to eat. Like the night before, Ryan began to wolf down the food, but then his chest began to heave and he put down his knife and fork.

'Tell us about yourself,' said Mum gently, and Ryan began to talk. About his Mum dying, about Joe getting drunk, not wanting him and finally hitting him. How he had to run away.

Mum got up and went to the kitchen to fetch the pudding. She called to Philip, and I put my finger to my lips and crept to the door to listen.

'You're just swayed by the resemblance,' Philip was saying.

'He's a child, Philip, and he's just lost his mother. He's alone and unhappy and scared. At least let's keep him until his future's sorted.'

I heard a heavy sigh. 'Have it your way,' Philip was saying, and I nipped back to my seat before the kitchen door opened.

Ryan

He liked Simon's Mum. She was kind and caring, like Mums should be. Like *his* Mum had been. After lunch she called him into the kitchen and asked him to help put things away.

'How d'you feel about this, Ryan – about you and Simon looking so alike?'

'I guess it's pretty amazing, but I suppose, like Simon said, we must be Doppelgangers. I expect there are others, maybe all over the world.'

'But how likely is it for them to meet each other? A bit of a miracle, isn't it?'

'I suppose so.'

'Do you have a photograph of your Mum, Ryan? Perhaps she and I look alike.'

'You don't,' he said, but he dug in his pocket and pulled out his wallet. He took out her picture and stared at the face he loved. A corner of the picture was creased and it was beginning to look worn and scuffed. He would have to find a better place for it.

He passed it to Simon's Mum. She looked at it for a long time. A *long* time.

'What was her name?'

'Maggie.'

She nodded. 'Nice name.' She passed the photograph back to him.

'Can you put the pans away, Ryan? In that bottom cupboard? I'm just popping upstairs.'

She looked a bit strange, a bit shocked.

'Is something wrong?' he asked.

'No, no. I've just remembered something I have to do.' But she didn't look at Ryan as she spoke.

He put the rest of the pans away and went back into the dining room.

Philip stood up. 'Another of the fences is down,' he said. 'You boys want to help me?'

Behind Philip's back Simon was shaking his head, but Ryan ignored him.

'Yes, please!' Although Ryan had helped Philip when he was hurt, he knew it wasn't enough. He had to do more. He had to do everything he could to make Philip like him, maybe like him even more than Simon, and then he would let him be part of his family. Let him live at the farm forever.

'Well! I'm glad one of you is interested!' said Philip. He looked over at Simon. 'You coming too?'

'No thanks.'

ELEVEN

Simon

When Ryan came down for breakfast the next morning, I watched him fill a bowl to the rim with cereal and pile his plate high with toast. He saw me looking, and paused, his hand in mid-air.

'It's alright, Ryan. There's plenty,' said Mum, giving me a warning glance.

After we'd finished eating, she tried to get him talking.

'So, what do you think of the farm, Ryan?'

'It's brilliant!'

'What d'you like best?'

'The animals, except – well, the bull was a bit scary!'

'He's a softie most of the time, but you should be a bit careful when you approach him. He'll get used to you.' She passed him the plate of toast and he took his fourth piece.

'Did you have any pets at home?'

He shook his head.

'Not even a cat or a dog?'

'When Mum and me lived in Cornwall we only ever had an apartment. No pets allowed. And Joe never wanted one. He said they were too much of a nuisance.'

'So you lived in Cornwall. I thought I detected a slight accent,' said Mum. 'When did you move to Liverpool?'

'It was after Mum met Joe. I think I was eight.'

'Well, there are plenty of animals here,' said Philip. 'Cows, sheep, chickens, the odd pig or two, a few geese,. When Simon first came here he got chased by a goose. He wouldn't come out of his bedroom for the rest of the day!'

I flushed, embarrassed, but Ryan laughed – for the first time since we met.

'Oh my God!' said Mum. 'Your teeth!'

Ryan flushed. 'What about them?'

'Philip, look! They're just like Simon's!'

I'd always been a bit self-conscious about my teeth. The incisors either side of my four upper front teeth are longer than the rest. At my new school some of the boys had started calling me Wolf Man.

Now I saw that Ryan's teeth were the same.

'I told you,' I said. 'He's my Doppelganger!'

But Philip was shaking his head.

'This is going beyond coincidence. You two are mirror images!' He turned to Mum. 'When you were growing up in Liverpool, did you have any other relatives? Aunts and uncles? Cousins?'

She shook her head. 'None that I knew of. There was just my mother's sister in London, my Aunt

Deborah. She took me in after Simon was born. But she never married and she didn't have children. I never heard of any other relatives.'

'What about you, Ryan?' asked Philip. 'Do you have any family? Anywhere around here?'

'No. Me and my Mum, we'd always lived in Cornwall. She never talked about any relatives.'

'What about your father?'

'He was in the merchant navy, she told me. First Mate on a ship, and he got drowned before I was born, so they never got married. I've never even seen a photo of him.'

'What was his name?'

'David something. I don't know if she ever told me his last name.'

'But it would be on your birth certificate?'

'Maybe. I've never seen it.'

'So your mother brought you up all on her own?'

'Until she met Joe. Mum worked at a hotel in Newquay and Joe came there one summer and got a job as a porter.'

'So, McKenna is *her* surname. Shouldn't be too difficult to trace, not like Smith.'

'Or Jones, or Brown, or Green, or Black,' said Lissie. I rolled my eyes and she glowered at me.

Mum got up from the table and collected our cereal bowls. She came back from the kitchen with a bowl of fresh raspberries and more toast. Ryan's eyes widened and I wondered if he'd ever stop feeling hungry. Mum pushed the plate towards him.

'Why did you move to Liverpool, Ryan?' she asked.

'Joe's was just a summer job. His home was here, and when the job finished we moved back with him.'

'So your Mum had no connections here at all. No relatives,' said Philip.

'I never met any.' Ryan was silent for a while. 'Mum didn't really like it here. We never went out much. Joe used to go to work and meet his mates at the pub in the evening, but Mum and me mostly stayed home.'

Philip sighed. 'Well, I'm beaten.' He gazed at Ryan and me in turn. 'Must be just a quirk of nature. What did you say were the odds, Simon? One in three trillion?'

'What about Mr Geoghegan? I could phone him,' said Mum. 'He might know more. He might even have Ryan's birth certificate.'

'No!' Ryan pushed himself away from the table. 'Please don't. He might want to take me back!'

'Do you really think so?'

'No – yes – I don't know. Maybe – '

Mum reached out and squeezed his hand. 'We will have to speak to him at some stage, Ryan. Even if he's not your official guardian, he's looked after you for years. But I'm sure he won't mind you staying here for a while – at least until we can sort things out.'

Ryan didn't say anything more. He turned his head away, but not before I could see a tear trickling down his cheek.

Ryan

Ryan was scared. What if Joe refused to give him up? He might decide Ryan could be useful. He might even ask for money to help support him. That would be embarrassing. If that happened, Ryan knew he would have to run away again.

Or Joe might ask for money *not* to take him back, and that would be even more embarrassing. He would feel like a parcel, to be bought and sold. And he might never know if Simon's mother and Philip were just trying to protect him or if they really wanted him. He wanted them, and already – he couldn't help it – he was beginning to feel part of their family, but how did they feel? How did they *really* feel?

Please don't phone Joe, he prayed. But after lunch Caro picked up the phone and keyed in Joe's number. It rang and rang, until she sighed and put the phone down.

'He's not there.'

Simon

That evening Mum started again, despite Ryan's pleading.

'We need to know more about you, Ryan. Your school, your health – and we do need his permission for you to stay here, Ryan. Otherwise we might have the police calling again.'

'You don't. He's not my guardian, and he and my Mum didn't even get married. He just put up with me because I was her son.'

'Well, we need permission from someone,' said Philip. 'If not from him, then from Social Services.

They'd want to make sure we're fit to look after you. Even if it's only temporarily.'

Ryan was quiet.

'Do we have to tell them?' asked Lissie. 'Can't we just keep Ryan here and hide him away if anyone comes?'

'Of course not,' said Philip.

'So what do we do?' asked Mum.

'We contact Social Services,' said Philip. 'And in the meantime we can send away for a copy of Ryan's birth certificate.'

'And if he turns out to be a cousin or something,' I asked, 'does that mean we can keep him?'

'Not necessarily,' said Philip, and I wasn't sure if that was because of the vetting thing, or because he didn't want to commit himself to Ryan living here permanently.

'Well, I'm going to try Mr Geoghegan once more,' said Mum. And this time she was successful.

'Ah! Mr Geoghegan!' She put on a big smile, even though he couldn't see her, and that soft purring voice that usually got everyone saying Yes to her. Five minutes later she had it all arranged.

'He's coming round,' she told us. She reached out and caught Ryan's arm as he started to rush out of the room. 'It's alright, Ryan. I'd like you to be here, but I promise you I won't let him take you away – not today, and we'll do our best to ensure that he can't take you unless you agree to it.'

I'm not sure Ryan was convinced, but he let her hug him, and he sat down to wait.

'Simon,' said Philip. 'I think you should leave this to us. I think I'd rather he didn't see you.'

'Why not?' I demanded.

'Let's just keep it simple. For now,' he said. 'Lissie, I'd rather you stayed upstairs. I don't want you involved. And Simon, please keep out of sight. I'll call you if you're needed.'

'That's not fair!' said Lissie, as we went upstairs. 'Why you and not me?'

I shrugged. I wondered what Philip was planning.

It was another twenty minutes before Mr Geoghegan's car, a shabby old Ford, drove slowly up the drive. I waited until Philip had let him in and taken him into the sitting room and then put my finger to my lips and began to creep down the stairs, Lissie following me. The door to the sitting room was very slightly ajar.

Mum was talking. 'We're so pleased to have found your son, Mr Geoghegan.'

'Not my son. My late partner's son,' he said.

'Of course,' she agreed, 'but I'm sure you're concerned for him.'

'We found him sheltering in an old cottage on the edge of our farm,' said Philip.

'He's such a nice boy,' said Mum. 'We'd like to help. I understand his mother died recently and he's very upset. We'd be happy to have him stay with us for a while, but only if you agreed, of course?'

There was quite a long silence, and then Mr Geoghegan spoke. 'How long did you have in mind?'

'Well – what do *you* think, Mr Geoghegan?' asked Philip.

'An unpaid hand - I suppose he could be quite useful to you on the farm?'

Philip's voice became very quiet and cold.

'I can afford to pay for help when I need it, Mr Geoghegan.'

'Him and me,' said Mr Geoghegan. 'We haven't been close. Maybe he'd be better off here – but, of course, I'd be losing money. Child Allowance, and so on . . . ? Not sure if I can spare him.'

'So – Am I hearing correctly, Mr Geoghegan? You'd be happy to sell him to us?'

There was another, even longer, silence, and then the sitting room door was pulled open. I'd had my ear to it and almost fell in.

'Come in, Simon.' Philip waved Lissie away. I saw her indignant face. I felt quite sorry for her.

'This is *my* son,' said Mum to Mr Geoghegan.

I'd never seen anyone turn white before. Actually, Mr Geoghegan's face wasn't really white. It was more a very pale shade of pinky green. He groped behind him and collapsed into a chair.

'Oh God! Oh God!' he whispered. His eyes switched backwards and forwards, backwards and forwards, between Ryan and me, and then between Ryan and my Mum.

'It's you, isn't it?' he said to her.

What did he mean? No one said anything. Mum was looking quite pale. The silence seemed to go on and on, and then at last Mum spoke.

'Do you have something more to tell us, Mr Geoghegan?'

It took a while. But then he began to speak.

'I didn't know anything about it until Maggie took ill. When she got the first diagnosis she thought she was going to die there and then – and she started worrying about Ryan. What would happen to him.'

He was sweating. He took out a handkerchief and wiped his face.

'She told me. About being a sort of unofficial midwife when she was in her twenties. She'd had some training at one of the Liverpool hospitals. Never finished, but it was enough to set her up to help those who didn't want others to know about their pregnancies, mostly young girls who didn't want their parents to know. It was hard for her. She'd been told she could never have children herself, but helping others, holding their babies – it was the next best thing.'

Mum turned to Philip. 'Ryan showed me the photograph of his mother,' she said. 'I thought she looked familiar, and now I know why. She was the woman who helped me.'

'You were the first one with twins. She said you'd never have coped, you were only seventeen and the boy, the father, wasn't any older. And you didn't even know you were expecting two! She thought she'd be doing you a favour, see?'

Twins! Ryan and me? Ryan's face had turned white, and Mum was swaying. Philip reached out and grabbed her.

Mr Geoghegan was still talking, his words coming

faster and faster. 'She said you were really out of it – she'd given you something for the pain - so she hid one of the babies away. Gave him a bottle - put him in a drawer in another room - got you and the other one away. And after that she packed up, took herself and the baby – Ryan – away to where no one knew her.'

No one said anything for a while. We were all stunned. I think Mum would have fallen over if Philip hadn't been holding her.

'You knew all this and you didn't go to the police?' he asked.

'I couldn't tell anyone,' said Mr Geoghegan. 'And I couldn't leave her, not when she was so ill. And after she died – well, it was too late then, wasn't it?'

'All these years . . . All these years I've had another son.' Mum's voice was barely more than a whisper. 'All these years. How could it be possible? How could I not have known?' She was crying now, and Philip pulled her closer. He glared at Mr Geoghegan.

'You should have told the police. As soon as you knew -'

'Would *you* have told? Would you have turned in your wife there, someone you loved, for kidnapping and a jail sentence? If I'd known right at the beginning – I wouldn't have told on her, but I mightn't have stayed, because I would have got in trouble as well, wouldn't I? Aiding and abettting. But when she was ill – well, I stayed and I kept silent. But Ryan there – I couldn't let myself care about him.'

'I don't understand,' said Philip. 'How did she get away with it?'

'She left Liverpool right away. Just packed up and took the train to Cornwall. She'd lived there as a girl and loved the place.'

'But what about documents?'

'She registered his birth in Cornwall. Herself as mother, and father unknown.'

'That's not right.' Ryan's face was as pale as Joe's. 'See, he's lying. She told me my father was in the navy.'

Joe shook his head. 'She made him up when you were old enough to ask questions. She thought you'd find that exciting.'

'You're lying! All of you, you're lying! My Mum was good, she would never do all those things. She wouldn't!' He was sobbing, huge sobs, choking with them. 'She wouldn't, she wouldn't!'

None of us knew what to say. We just stood there, helpless, waiting as he shook with the storm of his tears. They seemed to go on forever, but at last they stopped. His eyes were red and swollen, his face wet and snotty. He wiped his sleeve across it.

'You're making it up, all of you,' he whispered when he was able to speak again. 'She loved me and I loved her. She wouldn't! Just so that – so that – I don't know – What do you want from me?'

Mum broke away from Philip and ran to him then.

'Oh, my poor boy! My poor boy!' She flung her arms around him. 'It's going to be alright. You're my boy and I'm your mother, and I promise I will always look after you!'

Ryan wrenched himself free and backed away. 'No!

You're not my mother! You're not! I've got a mother – she's dead, but she's still my mother, not you! Not you!'

TWELVE

Simon

After Mr Geoghegan had gone and Ryan had rushed up to his bedroom, Lissie crept in, her face a mix of resentment at having been shut outside and excitement at the idea of Ryan becoming one of the family. Mum had huddled into a corner of the sofa, her face white and her eyes closed. I had no idea what she was thinking. Philip was frowning and I guessed he was trying to work out what to do next – and maybe not too happy at the thought that he might now be stuck with not just one of me, but two. None of us knew what to say to each other.

As for me – I couldn't really take it in. I had never even considered that Ryan might be my twin. I mean – how could a woman have two babies without her knowing? Even if she'd been knocked out? She would have seen doctors, had scans at the hospital, wouldn't she? But maybe Mum hadn't. Perhaps she just hid away from everyone until we were born.

Was I pleased? I think so. Or was I? This was all too sudden.

Lissie crept over and sat beside me. She looked as shocked as all of us, and I could see she was near to tears. I put my arm round her and she moved closer.

'Should I go up and see him?' I asked Mum.

'No. I don't think that's a good idea right now. And he won't want to see me,' she whispered. 'But maybe – Lissie, you might be the best person at the moment. You could take him some hot milk?'

'Yes!'

Ryan

Ryan slammed his bedroom door and, still dressed, flung himself on to the bed and pulled the duvet up to his ears.

He didn't believe any of it. Mum wouldn't have, *couldn't have,* done any of the things they'd talked about. Joe was lying. It was just a scheme to make money, to dump him on someone else, and now they were all involved, even Simon's mother, who had been so nice to him.

Telling him that she was his real mother! That was evil, and he wanted to hate her for it. Surely she didn't believe what Joe had told her. They were all saying awful things about his Mum, who had loved and cared for him for thirteen years, all of his life, and was no longer here to defend herself.

Someone knocked on the door.

'Go away!'

The knock came again.

'It's me. Lissie. Can I come in?'

'No!' he called, but she came in anyway.

'I've brought you some hot milk, but I've put some chocolate in it. Can I stay?' She didn't wait for an answer but perched on the side of his bed.

He turned his back on her. She was part of the enemy now and he waited for her to leave, but she didn't.

'I've lost my Mum too. It's rotten, isn't it?'

Whatever, it couldn't be as bad as being told your mother was a kidnapper and a criminal.

'Go away!' he hissed again, but still she stayed.

He gave in. 'Alright, what happened to her?'

'She met another man, an American, and she went to live in San Francisco. That's over 3000 miles away from Liverpool. I don't think she'll ever come back. Sometimes my Dad says bad things about her when he doesn't know I'm there – and even though she never contacts me, that still hurts.'

'Well, no-one's going to say bad things about *my* Mum!'

'I don't think Caroline will. She'll understand.' Lissie picked up the mug. 'Don't you want this?'

'No! I don't want anything *she's* made for me.'

'Actually, *I* made it, but if you don't want it - ' She took a swig. 'Mmm. Nice!'

Ryan pulled the duvet over his ears but he could still hear her.

'There's nothing that says you can't have two Mums. Lots of girls in my school have had more than one. One girl's had four. *Four!* So Caroline's my second Mum, and she's really kind and she lets me talk about my real Mum, my birth Mum, and she never says bad things about her. It'd be just the same for you, except it's the other way round. Caroline's your actual birth Mum and your other, your Cornish mum, was the one who cared for you and loved you afterwards.'

He wished she would go away. Maybe what Lissie said made sense, but even to listen to her made him feel disloyal. He closed his eyes and pulled the duvet even higher. Eventually he heard her open the door and leave.

Simon

From my bedroom later I could hear the murmur of Mum's and Philip's voices way into the night. I couldn't sleep.

From a three trillion to one chance to actually being a twin! It felt so weird. I supposed it could have been even more weird. Mum could have had triplets. Or quads. Or even quintuplets. There was a case that was in the news once of a woman having eight babies all at once!

I was picturing seven other kids who all looked like me when I eventually fell asleep.

I awoke when Lissie barged into my room the next day. I peered at my alarm. Seven o'clock.

'He's gone!' Lissie cried. 'He's packed all his stuff and he's gone!'

She ran out of the room, and then came back.

'And he's taken your bike!'

What? My bike? For a moment I felt really angry, and then I remembered I'd promised he could have it if he ever needed to run away again.

'Where's Mum? What's she doing?'

She's on the phone to the police. She thinks he

probably left hours ago and with your bike he could have got quite a long way. She phoned Mr Geoghegan but there was no reply.'

'What's Philip doing?'

'He's gone to check the cottage.'

'Ryan won't have gone back there.' I felt a bit sick. Just as things might be turning out well for Ryan, he decides to run away. OK, so he was upset about his Mum. *I* would be if I found out the Mum I'd known for thirteen years wasn't my Mum at all and could have gone to prison if anyone had found out -but *my* Mum, who's now *his* Mum too, would take care of him, and love him, if he'd give her a chance. Maybe just a three week trial would have done it. Everyone likes my Mum.

I went downstairs. Mum was still on the phone to the police station.

'Yes, he's only thirteen. When I got up this morning, I saw his bed was empty. He's on a bike, so he could have gone quite a distance.'

What's his full name?'

Mum hesitated and then she glanced at me and put her finger to her lips.

'His name is Simon. Simon Hendricks.'

'Why did you use *my* name?' I asked after the call was finished.

'Because if I said it was Ryan, they'd probably take him straight to a hostel. They wouldn't let him come back here until they'd investigated – and as he'd most likely say he didn't want to come here, that would be the end of it.'

'But he *is* your son.'

'I believe that, and you believe it, but there's still no actual proof, and he probably still has the right to refuse to live with me.'

I phoned Melanie. 'He's gone again,' I told her. 'Taken my bike and rushed off to who knows where. Have you heard from him?'

There was a gasp from her end of the line. 'Oh no! What happened?'

I told her. I think she dropped her phone in the middle of it but in the silence that followed I could feel her shock. I started again and I asked if she had any idea where he might have gone. We decided he would be unlikely to go back to the park and neither of us could suggest anywhere else.

'He wouldn't come back here,' she said. 'And anyway, Joe's not here. My Dad was up at six and he saw him putting all these suitcases and boxes – loads of them, clothes, books, kitchen stuff – into his car. My Dad thinks he's done a bunk!'

Melanie sighed. 'Can I come round to yours later?'

'I suppose so. Maybe you could try Ryan on your phone first. He might answer if it's you.'

Mum was calling me.

'I've no idea where he could be heading,' I told her.

Philip was back. 'He's not at the cottage.'

'He wouldn't be. He hated it there. And Melanie said he's not back home, but she's going to call him. Oh, and she said Joe had packed up and gone.' I hesitated. 'I said she could come round here. Is that alright?'

'Of course,' said Philip, but he wasn't really listening. 'I'm not happy that Ryan stole your bike, Simon.'

'He didn't actually steal it,' I said. 'I told him if he was ever in trouble again he could take it.'

'Really?' Philip turned away, but not before I had seen the hurt on his face.

Ryan

He had been pedalling for at least an hour and a half, mile after mile, through places he'd never seen before. The traffic was thickening. He was hungry. And thirsty. He should have grabbed some food and drink before he left.

They would be having breakfast back at the farm. He recalled the breakfast he had eaten the previous day and his mouth watered as he pictured them all at the table. Caroline and Philip would be eating hot porridge with brown sugar sprinkled over, then thick cream from their own cows..... Simon and Lissie would most likely have Coco Pops. Then there would be toast with Caroline's home-made raspberry jam, or marmalade so thick and chunky that you had to spoon it on.

He realised he had no money on him. Not a single coin. Luckily his phone was still charged up. He had pedalled past a children's playground. No children there, of course, it was far too early. He dismounted from the bike and wheeled it through the gate.

There was only one person he could call. Melanie.

'Oh, Ryan! Simon told me you'd run away. Why?

It's where you belong now, and they want you, don't they?'

'They told me my Mum had stolen me when I was born. That she'd have gone to prison if anyone had known. That Caroline is my real Mum – and I don't believe it. My Mum was good and kind, and she would never hurt anyone by stealing a baby from them!'

He tried to swallow the hard lump in his throat. His nose was running. He swiped it with the back of his hand.

'It's not true. They were lying, all of them!'

'Oh Ryan!'

Simon

Melanie didn't turn up, but the police – Bill again – did. I listened from the kitchen as Mum told him that Simon – me! - had disappeared, following an argument. Lissie was with me in the kitchen and started to speak. I put my finger to her mouth and she glared at me but was silent.

'He might come back of his own accord,' said Mum, 'but he's so young, and he must have gone in the early hours. Anything could happen. He took his bike, but I don't think anything else has gone – food, money, clothes. And it's raining, too. I'm really worried.'

'Well, I'll put out an alarm,' said Bill. 'At least I know what he looked like. What was he wearing?

'I've no idea. None of us saw him leave. I don't even know if he took a jacket.'

'What sort of bicycle?'

'Erm – Philip?'

'Oh, a Piranha, I think. Pretty new.'

I'll get you a photograph of him,' said Mum.

'Well,' said Philip, when Bill had gone. 'I must say, you're a good liar, Carrie!'

'When necessary,' she said, but then her face crumpled. 'I'm worried about him, Philip. I really upset him last night – I didn't handle things very well.'

'He's just very sensitive – and loyal to the woman who stole him from you.'

'Of course he is, and if he'd just come back, I'm sure we could talk things through,' she said.

'He was really angry last night,' said Lissie. 'Didn't even drink the hot chocolate I made for him. I had to drink it instead.'

'Greedy guts!' I taunted.

'Misery guts!' she flung back.

'Stop it, you two,' said Mum. 'This is serious. Let's all put our heads together and think where he might be heading.'

It was then that Melanie called again.

'He's here! He's in Joe's house. Now Joe's gone, Ryan thinks he can hide out there, but he can't, can he? Someone will tell the Council, and anyway, they'll want someone to pay the rent, and anyway, Ryan's got no money for food or anything else – He can't – I told him -'

Mum took the phone from me. 'Melanie? It's alright, we'll come round, just give me the address – but keep him there! Don't tell him we're on our way!'

THIRTEEN

Simon

Bad timing. Philip's car had a flat tyre. We all bundled into Mum's little Fiat.

'There won't be room coming back,' I said. 'And what about the bike?'

Philip smiled. 'I thought you could ride it back, Simon.'

'Thanks!'

Melanie was at the window of Joe's house when we got there. It was just a little two up/two down terrace house, and there was barely room outside even for the Fiat, as all the neighbours' cars were still there from the night before.

Melanie rushed to open the front door. I could see my bike, parked in the narrow hall. Ryan was behind her.

'You told them!' he accused her.

'I had to,' she said. 'You know you can't stay here, Ryan.'

Ryan glared out at us. 'You can't make me leave.'

'We're not going to force you, Ryan,' said Philip, 'but Social Services won't let you live here on your own. How could you survive?'

'Melanie will help me.'

'I don't think I can,' said Melanie. 'Not here, with my Mum and Dad watching. *They* would call Social Services.'

I could see Ryan was trying not to cry.

'Please come,' said Lissie. 'We all want you to come and live with us, don't we, Mum?'

Ryan glared at her. '*You* can call her Mum, if you want – but she's not going to take *my* Mum's place, no one could. Go away, all of you!' And he pushed Melanie outside and slammed the front door.

Philip shrugged his shoulders. 'Come on.' He glanced at his watch. 'I'm hungry. Anyone fancy fish and chips?'

Mum was shocked. 'We can't just abandon him!'

'It's what he wants. Come on, back in the car,' he said, but he was winking at us as he said it. He spoke a few words to Melanie and then he joined us. We left her standing on the pavement, looking bewildered.

We found the local fish and chip shop down one of the side streets and took the hot greasy packages back to the car. Philip had bought an extra portion and had it double wrapped.

'Eat up,' he said. 'We don't want this one to get cold.'

'Is that - ?'

'For Ryan? Yes. I thought your Mum could take it to him. The rest of us can stay in the car.'

So there was no time to actually enjoy our lunch. We gobbled down our portions as quickly as we could, and then Philip started the car again. He parked near the top end of Ryan's street. Mum picked up the spare package and left us. We watched as she walked briskly towards Ryan's house.

'Do you think it will work?' I asked.

'I hope so. If anyone can persuade him, it's Caroline!'

Ryan

He was on his own. Even Melanie had gone back next door. He stood in the hall, feeling lonelier than he'd ever been in his life. The house had never felt so empty. Most of the furniture was still there, and the carpets which were old and stained, but Joe must have taken everything else.

He climbed the stairs and paused by the door into what had been Joe's and his Mum's bedroom. A memory flashed into his mind. His Mum lying in bed, her eyes huge and dark, her body barely making a dent in the bedclothes. The District Nurse had just left, and Joe had escaped to the pub. Mum had taken his hand, her own hand thin and bony.

'I'll never stop loving you,' she had whispered. 'My boy. If there's a Heaven, I'll be looking down on you, watching over you. My boy,' she whispered again. 'You won't forget me, will you?'

How could he ever forget her? But what would she want him to do? Here? Now?

He sat down on the floor, his forehead resting against the empty bed, and cried.

When the doorbell rang he ignored it, but it

wouldn't stop. Perhaps it was Melanie, back to keep him company. He had been angry with her, but none of this was her fault. She had tried to help him, right from the beginning, and he wished he hadn't snapped..

But it was not Melanie. It was *her*. Caroline. He tried to shut the door but she had put her foot in the way. She handed him the warm parcel.

'Fish and chips,' she said. 'You must be starving.'

He was. 'Thanks,' he muttered.

'Are you going to let me in? Whatever you decide, I think we should have a little talk first, don't you?'

He looked past her, down the street.

'It's alright. They're staying in the car. It's just you and me, and I promise that when we're finished I'll go away, if that's what you want.'

He could feel the warmth of the fish and chips through the wrapping, and he licked his lips. He didn't resist when she pushed gently against the door and stepped inside.

They sat at the small table in the kitchen. She was silent until he had finished and then she waited while he turned on the tap at the sink and cupped his hands to drink.

'I'll make you another promise,' she said when he came back to the table. 'I promise I won't try to take your Mum's place. I know how much you must have loved her. Just let me – us – look after you, at least until you're old enough to look after yourself.'

He couldn't speak. What would his Mum have wanted him to do?

As if reading his thoughts, Caroline spoke again.

'Do you think she would want you to be alone and unhappy? I think she'd hate that, don't you?'

Ryan nodded.

'I won't try to take her place. There's room for all kinds of love in life, and one doesn't necessarily take the place of another. They can live side by side. What did you call her, Ryan?'

'Mum, of course.'

'Well, I suppose you'd have to call me something. I've been looking up the Cornish for Mum, and it's Mamm. How about you use that for me? Or there are lots of other titles you could give me. When Simon first started learning German he called me Mutti for a while. I guess you could go through the dictionaries and find plenty of alternatives. I'd leave it up to you.' She smiled. 'Although nothing too rude or insulting, I hope?'

Ryan was silent for quite a time. 'I'll think about it,' he said at last.

'And *I* was thinking – do you still have her photograph?'

'Of course.'

'Well, I noticed it was very worn. Simon's good at restoring photos on his computer. He could do that for you – and I could buy a nice frame for it, and then you could have it in your room?'

He didn't answer for a long time, but at last he nodded.

She smiled. 'We all want you, Ryan. I hope you'll come back. It'll be OK, you'll see.'

She leaned back in her chair and waited, silent now, for him to give in.

And after a while he did.

'I'll get my stuff,' he said.

Simon

I pedalled as fast as I could on the way back. I knew Philip's car would get them there before me, but I didn't want to miss anything. Of course it started to rain and I didn't have a jacket, so I was a bit grumpy by the time I reached the farm.

They were all in the kitchen, drinking hot tea and stuffing themselves with cookies. Mum was sitting at one end of the long table, Philip at the other. Lissie and Ryan sat opposite each other. Philip was telling a story about a sheep that had wandered into the house one day. Even Ryan, with three cookies and a banana in front of him, was laughing.

I sat down next to Lissie and wondered why I felt so out of it. I had been so keen to find Ryan, to help him and protect him, but now . . . Now he was one of the family, and no one had even noticed I was back.

'Is there anything left for me?' I asked loudly, and Mum smiled, understanding. 'You haven't missed anything,' she said.

Lissie leaned towards me and whispered. 'You don't have to be jealous.'

Was that it? Was I just annoyed because Ryan was getting all the attention? Or was it because Ryan was no longer just a boy who looked like me, he was my twin, and from now on I would have to share my

Mum with him?

Mum got up from the table. As she passed my seat she put her hand on my shoulder. I looked up.

'I should phone the police,' she said. 'I'll need you to tell them you're back and you're ok.'

I followed her to the sitting room. She sat down on the sofa and patted the seat beside her.

'Aren't you going to phone?'

'In a minute. Tell me first what's making you unhappy.'

'I don't know. It's just – things are going to be different, aren't they?'

'But that's good, isn't it? I know you've been lonely since we moved here. I know you missed your friends in London, and you haven't really had time to make new ones. Finding Ryan – that's amazing, and you were the one who started it all, who persevered and helped him. All credit to you!'

I shrugged and turned my face away, my eyes suddenly stinging.

Mum put out a hand and turned me back to her. 'You're my dearly beloved son, Simon. I've loved you since the moment I opened my eyes and saw your tiny face next to me, and I've loved you for thirteen years. Nothing is going to change that.'

'But he'll be here and I'll be away at boarding school,' I said bitterly.

'Lissie'll be away, too.' She was silent for a while, her arm around my shoulders. 'I'm thinking, how would you feel about going to a local day school – all three of you?'

'That would be brilliant! Absolutely brilliant!'

'Alright, but don't say anything to the others until I've talked to Philip. But first I need to talk to the police. You'd better be ready to make an apology too.'

FOURTEEN

Ryan

He couldn't sleep. So much had happened in the past twenty four hours. Some of it he couldn't bear to think about. His Mum. What she had done. No! His Mum was a good person, she must have had her reasons. But what if – No, think of something else.

Lissie. She was nice, he liked her, and so had Melanie.

Philip was nice too. He was kind, and he had sorted out Joe. Philip was on his side.

Simon was on his side too, but something was wrong there. He didn't seem so friendly any more.

Then there was Caroline. He didn't know what to do about her. She'd been nice, she'd been kind, but she could never replace – he wouldn't *let* her replace - his Mum, his *real* Mum, never ever. She had suggested he call her Mutti. Could he bring himself to do that? Or should he just go on calling her Caroline?

He didn't want to think any more. And he was hungry. Would he *ever* stop feeling hungry? He got out of bed, put on the dressing gown that hung on the door, and crept down the stairs.

Just as he was about to open the kitchen door he heard their voices. Caroline and Simon.

'Don't you believe Mr Geoghegan's story?' Caroline was asking. 'You think he's lying?'

'No, I don't think he's lying.'

'Good, because *I'm* convinced. I *know* Ryan's my son, even though I don't remember the birth.'

'But you need to prove it if you don't want Social Services constantly checking on us and possibly even deciding to take him away – and the best way to do that is to have a DNA test. You, Simon and Ryan, all three of you.'

There was silence, a long one. And then Caroline spoke.

'Alright. Arrange it. I'll talk to the boys in the morning.'

Ryan tiptoed back to his room.

He knew about DNA tests, they were always cropping up in the detective series on Netflix, and they were always 100 per cent accurate.

If it proved he was related to Caroline and Simon, he would have to accept Joe's story and that his Mum had commited a crime. If it proved the opposite, then he would know for sure that his Mum was innocent, that she was his real Mum.

But did he want the test? Whatever it proved, he knew she was a good person and had loved him a thousand per cent. He had never doubted that.

Simon

The house was quiet when I woke up. Perhaps they were all exhausted after the excitement of the day before, but I'd found it hard to sleep. I threw on a sweatshirt and my jeans and crept downstairs. It was too early even to feel hungry for breakfast.

Philip was there, though, drinking coffee.

'Morning,' he said. 'I'm going to bring the cows in. Want to tag along?'

What? Surely he wasn't expecting me to help him? But he jerked his head and I followed him, out and across to the field where the cows were shifting uneasily. I could almost hear their sighs of relief when they saw Philip and there were several Moos of welcome.

'They get pretty uncomfortable when they're not milked promptly. Open the gate, will you?'

He began to usher the cows through the opening, and I followed behind.

I had never been inside the milking parlour, although both Mum and Philip had offered me a tour at different times. It was clean, almost sparkling, and pretty impressive really. I suppose I hadn't actually pictured Philip sitting on a bucket pulling teats, like in All Creatures Great and Small, but on the other hand I hadn't pictured it as like something in a car factory.

I watched him disinfecting the cows' teats, and then he showed me how the milking pipes were attached.

'Want to have a go?' he asked.

I stepped back, shocked.

'Scared?'

'Of course not!'

He watched as I fumbled with the pipes, still not sure which bits to attach to what, and thankful that the cow wouldn't be able to kick me. But I did it, and actually the cow, my cow, looked quite pleased once the milking began.

'How do you know when she's empty?' I asked, and he smiled.

When we'd finished and all the cows had been released and let out to pasture, he threw an arm around my shoulders.

'Thanks, Ryan.'

'I'm not Ryan,' I said. 'I'm Simon.'

'*Simon?*' His eyes widened and then he smiled. 'Well, thanks even more!'

I smiled back. I think it was probably the first time I'd pleased him, and if felt quite good.

But I still wanted to be an artist, not a farmer.

The others were at the breakfast table when we got back. Mum and Lissie were chatting about Lissie's coming birthday. Lissie had drawn up an invitation list, which was fairly small as, like me, her boarding school was too far away for termtime friends to visit. I wondered if Mum had spoken to Philip yet about us moving to local schools.

'So, what have you bought me?' Lissie beamed at me, half serious, and – again half serious – I scowled and said 'Nothing!' Actually, it was true, I barely had enough to buy her a birthday card. But I did have a present for her and it was almost finished. A full length portrait of her holding her favourite chicken, which I'd painted in oils from a photograph I'd taken on the sly. But Ryan was looking quite gloomy, hunched up in his chair with an uneaten bowl of cereal in front of him. Of course, he didn't have any money to buy anything, and I wondered if Philip would start an account for him, like he'd done for me. I wondered how it felt to find yourself in a strange house with a new family, your old one being dead. And nothing of your own, not even money.

I asked Mum if Melanie could come round later, thinking it might cheer him up. She said yes, and his face brightened, but after the breakfast things had been cleared she said that she and Philip had something to discuss with us.

'I think we need to tell the police that you're living here now, Ryan. But they might still feel they have to involve Social Services to make sure we're suitable to look after you. So, we think you, Simon and I should have a DNA test.'

'Me too?' asked Lissie.

'No, dear. The test is just to prove I'm Ryan's mother – his *birth* mother, I mean,' she added as Ryan stood up and backed away from the table.

'No! You just want to prove my Mum was wicked - a criminal! I won't have one, and you can't make me!'

'Please, Ryan, sit down. I don't think your mother – Maggie – was wicked. Yes, what she did was a crime, but I don't think she ever meant to hurt anyone. If she longed for a baby of her own, I can see her reasoning and how she just seized the opportunity. I was seventeen, and terrified. My own mother was dead and my father was very strict with me. My boyfriend was only eighteen, he was starting at university in the Autumn, and the last thing he wanted was to be tied down with a baby.'

Mum turned to Lissie. 'Lissie, you don't need to hear all this.'

'Yes, I do! You don't need to treat me like *I'm* a baby. I'm almost twelve, practically old enough to have a baby myself!'

'Don't you dare!' said Philip, rolling his eyes.

'So I'd been hiding the pregnancy under lots of loose clothes, and I'd been stuffing myself with food, ballooning all over. I hadn't been near a doctor or a hospital, and I couldn't tell my father. Just one girlfriend knew, and she told me about Maggie,' said Mum. 'I went to her house when it came time to have the baby. I had no idea I was expecting twins.'

'But you must have realised when – when it started?'

'I was so scared, and – it hurt. I could have given birth to a cage full of monkeys and not realised. Maggie gave me something to help, and it more or less knocked me out. But I'd told her my circumstances and she would have known I couldn't possibly cope with two – one was going to be hard enough!'

She leaned across the table and caught Ryan's hand. ' And now, well, she's dead, Ryan, so nothing's going to hurt her.'

No one spoke. Mum must have told Philip all this when they first got together, and I knew that she'd been still a schoolgirl when I was born, but that's all. Lissie looked near to tears, and Philip moved over and put his arm round her.

Ryan? He was really pale. He looked frozen to his seat, and he wouldn't look at any of us. Then suddenly he stood up, his chair falling over, and rushed off to his room.

I stood up. 'Shall I -'

'No. Leave him,' said Mum. 'We'll talk again at lunch.'

But lunchtime came and Ryan was still in his room. Mum sent Lissie to fetch him.

'He doesn't want anything,' she said on her return.

'Well, that's a first,' said Philip, but Mum started to fill a plate. 'Take it in, Lissie. He may just prefer to be on his own.'

Later, when we had finished, I knocked on Ryan's door. There was no reply but I went in anyway. He was lying on his bed and his eyes were red again.

'Melanie should be here soon,' I said. 'We could go for a walk if you like.'

'I'd rather see her on my own.'

'You're still blaming my Mum, aren't you? That's not fair -'

'Do you know anything about my father?' he interrupted.

'*Our* father. No, only that he was in the year above her at school.' I waited but he said nothing more.

I shrugged. 'Suit yourself.'

Finding you had a twin brother should have been fun. Instead, it was upsetting the whole family. I wish I'd never seen that photograph in the newspaper.

Ryan

'I don't know what to do,' he told Melanie.

'Stay, that's what you must do – and have the DNA test. What would your Mum have said, if she'd known

Joe would dump you and you'd be all alone?'

'I know, but – What if it all comes out, and people start calling her a thief and a monster?'

'Ryan, she's not here any more. Nothing people say now can hurt her. And if she could know, wouldn't she be pleased that you've got a new family who will care about you?' Melanie glanced at the photograph of Maggie beside Ryan's bed. 'And I see they don't mind you keeping a photo of her? That looks quite new.'

'Simon cleaned it up on his computer, and Caroline gave me the frame.'

'You see? They're not trying to make you forget her. They're good people. I like them.' Melanie stood up. 'Now come on. Come and show me round the farm. I want to see everything.'

Ryan began to feel a little better as they walked across the farmyard, stopping to check out the chickens and the half dozen geese that Philip kept. Lissie called them as they opened the gate into the field of sheep. They waited as she ran to catch them up. He didn't mind. Liking Lissie didn't make him feel disloyal to his Mum, and anyway, Lissie had enough problems with her own mother. Besides, Melanie liked her. That was good enough for him.

They reached the field with the bull. 'Sidney!' Lissie called, and the bull lifted his head and began lumbering across the field to the fence. She leaned across and stroked his nose.

'Funny name for a bull,' said Melanie.

'All the bulls here have been called Sidney,' said Lissie. 'After my great-grandfather. My Dad said he was a huge man, and that was *his* name.'

'You're lucky, Ryan,' said Melanie, when they had finished their tour. 'You're going to be part of all this.'

Ryan reached out and stroked Sidney's nose, as Lissie had done. The bull accepted the caress and Ryan felt a thrill of pleasure.

'My Dad's ordered some DNA tests,' said Lissie. 'To prove he's one of us, and so Social Services can't take him away.'

'Won't make any difference,' Ryan said quickly. 'If I want to leave, I'll leave.'

'And go where?' asked Melanie.

'I don't know.'

'And what about school? We're due back soon.'

'I expect my Dad will send Ryan to the same school as Simon,' said Lissie.

'The boarding school? Simon said he got beaten every day.'

'He was joking. I think it's quite a good school. It's where my Dad went when he was young.'

'I'm not going!' said Ryan.

'But you have to go somewhere,' said Melanie, 'and they won't take you back in our school now you don't live round there.'

Ryan felt himself choking up. Just when he thought things might be improving, here was something else to worry about.

'I'm going back,' he said, and set off at a fast pace towards the house.

Melanie and Lissie looked at each other.

'He and his – his Mum were really close,' said

Melanie. 'Now she's gone, he's not really thinking straight about anything.'

'I know,' said Lissie. 'I was a bit like that when my Mum went off to America, but at least I still had my Dad.'

'Well, I think Ryan's lucky to have you all. He just doesn't know it yet.'

FIFTEEN

Simon

The appointments for the DNA tests came in the post.

'I thought we'd be able to do them at home,' said Mum.

'Not for paternity or maternity tests,' said Philip. 'Too much risk of fakery. We have to attend a DNA Clinic, and provide documents and photographs.'

'But I can come, can't I?' pleaded Lissie.

'Of course. Maybe we'll make a day of it. Lunch out. Some shopping. Not long till your birthday, Lissie,' said Mum.

Ryan said nothing. I hoped he wasn't planning to run away again.

But later he came to my room.

'About Lissie,' he said. 'I should give her something, shouldn't I? But I don't have any money.'

'Philip will give you some. I expect he just hasn't thought about it yet.'

'I don't want his money.' He stared around the room. 'What are you giving her?'

My easel was facing the wall but I turned it round.

'I'm painting her portrait from a photo. That's Petronella, her favourite chicken that she's hugging.'

He stared at the painting for a long time. 'You're really good, aren't you?'

I shrugged. 'Not bad, I suppose. I do enjoy it.'

'Maybe - I mean, I can't paint portraits and stuff. I'm not a proper artist, but I like drawing Manga comics.'

'Really? That's great. It's still art, something we've got in common!'

'Maybe I could create one for Lissie, with her as the heroine. What do you think?'

'I think she'd be absolutely amazed. Fantastic! It would probably be her favourite birthday present.'

He stood there, shuffling a bit. 'Erm – I don't suppose you've got a spare sketch pad? And maybe some acrylic inks and pens?'

'I'll have a look.'

I opened the cupboard where I kept all my art materials. I had several sketch pads in there, including one really expensive sketchbook, leather covered, with a strap and buckle , and a pocket on the cover to insert a name card or title. I hesitated. I had been saving it for something special, but this was it, wasn't it? I added a box of coloured inks, and some pens and brushes.

'Will this do?'

He nodded. 'Thanks.'

'Ryan,' I called as he was leaving.'I'm glad we share *something.*'

He shrugged again but – was that a half smile? Yes,

it was.

'I've invited my Aunt Deborah,' said Mum that night. 'She'll be here for your birthday, Lissie.'

'Oh, good!' said Lissie. 'You'll like her, Ryan. She's quite old, but she's lots of fun.'

'Aunt Deborah lives in London. She took care of me and Simon after the birth, and I lived with her for several years, until Simon was old enough for school and I could find a good job and a place of my own.'

'Does she know about me?' asked Ryan.

'Yes, I've told her. She's looking forward to meeting you.'

'Does she know - ?'

'Yes, but she feels the same as all of us.' Mum leaned forward and took Ryan's hand. 'We all want you to be part of this family.'

I saw Ryan blink away tears. I wished he wouldn't cry so much. I just wanted him to settle down and enjoy being with us. Most of all I suppose I wanted him to like *me*.

'She'll be driving up in her motor caravan, so I won't even have to prepare a bedroom for her. She goes all over the country in it, Ryan. Europe, too, all on her own. She's very brave.'

'She wears all these weird clothes,' said Lissie. 'And lots of make up, and lots of hair, all pinned up until it all starts falling down. Last time she came, we were finding pins in the carpets and down the back of chairs for ages after she left!'

'She's a teacher,' said Mum. 'Drama. Her kids love her.'

'Talking about teachers,' said Philip, 'there's

something we need to discuss. The holidays end soon, and Ryan, if you're allowed to stay with us, we'll have to find a new school for you. If it's not too late I'm prepared to enrol you in Simon's boarding school -'

'No!'

'I didn't think so. Well, Caroline suggested that we find a local school for you. I've looked around, and there's an independent day school just four or five miles from here which still has vacancies. What do you think?'

'Can't I go too?' I asked. 'You wouldn't want to split us, would you?'

He sighed. 'I'm sorry you didn't enjoy my old school. My father, my grandfather and my great grandfather were all pupils, and I loved it.'

'*I'm* sorry. It's just – I felt out of place, and I had no friends.'

'Dad,' said Lissie. 'I'd like to go to a day school too – if you don't mind. All three of us together – it would be lovely!'

'Ryan?'

He was silent for several minutes. He turned to Mum. 'What if the DNA test shows I'm not – not your son?' he asked Mum.

'We would still want you to stay here. You're part of this family now. No escape!'

And there it was again. That half smile. Ryan was beginning to accept us.

Philip was on to it the next morning. And in the afternoon he and Mum took us to view the new school, an easy bike ride from the farm. Redmond House, a big old mansion – Georgian, said Philip -

surrounded by lawns and flower beds and huge trees. In the distance, I could see playing fields and tennis courts. No kids, of course, we'd have to wait for the new term to meet them, but we met the Headmaster and his secretary, and they were really friendly and showed us round all the classrooms. Up on the top floor there were two large art studios. *Two*. That settled it for me. Lissie was impressed too. Ryan wasn't giving anything away, but at least he didn't look unhappy.

Ryan
Back home Ryan rushed off to his room. He had written a DO NOT DISTURB notice and he hung it on the door, although he had already noticed that the family were all good about allowing each other to be private. He took out the sketchbook, pens and inks that Simon had given him. It was time to start on Lissie's story.

But once he'd chosen his pens and brushes and set out all the colours, he paused. *How do I feel?* he asked himself. He closed the sketchbook. Was he being disloyal to his Mum, his *real* Mum, if he felt a little bit excited by the new school? Or because he was looking forward to creating a nice present for Lissie, who would perhaps soon be his sort-of sister? Or because he was starting to like Caroline, Simon's mother and most likely *his* mothe*r?* And Philip, soon to become his stepfather? Even Simon, who had started it all?

And there was an Aunt – or Great-Aunt, he supposed she would be – who sounded fun. And there was Lissie's birthday to look forward to. With

Melanie and maybe Jasmine there too. And he liked his room. And the farm. The animals, even Sidney, the bull.

And then there was the food.

'I'm sorry, MaggieMum,' he whispered. *'But I'll always love you best. I'll never let anything change how I feel about you.'*

He opened the sketchbook again, and picked up a pen.

Simon

There was an hour to spare before dinner. I left Lissie on the phone to Aunt Deborah, all excited at the prospect of her being there for her birthday, and went back to my room. Perhaps I'd be able to finish the portrait before Mum called us downstairs.

I stared at the painting. I think I'd caught Lissie's expression – the one she reserved for Petronella, sort of soppy. I quite enjoyed painting the chicken too, getting a golden sheen on the red feathers and a silvery green sheen on the black ones. Lissie would be pleased, I was sure.

I thought about Ryan, who was probably working on his Manga comic right now. I hoped it would turn out well and that Lissie would like it.

As long as she didn't like it better than my present.

At dinner that night everyone was relaxed and cheerful, even Ryan managing to produce a few smiles, and Philip seemed to have got over his disappointment that I didn't like his old school. I'd heard Mum telling him that at least he'd be saving money by sending us all to a day school, so that probably helped.

Lissie was sitting across the table from Ryan, and I noticed him watching her quite a lot between mouthfuls. She noticed and put down her fork.

'Why are you staring at me like that?' She rubbed her face. 'Have I got food on it?'

'I wasn't staring,' said Ryan. 'I was just thinking.'

'Well, I wish you'd look at something else while you think. You're making me feel weird!'

I guessed he was memorising her features for his comic. I had several photographs of her filed away in my desk. I would take them to his room when we went up to bed.

After dinner we watched a really scary film about strange creatures breeding in the drains.

'I'm going to have nightmares,' said Lissie.

'No you won't, said Mum. 'Just remember to put plugs in all the washbowls – and lids down on the loos, you boys!'

At breakfast the next morning Philip reminded us that we'd be visiting the DNA Clinic later that day. I glanced at Ryan. He had been cramming Coco Pops into his mouth, and he stopped mid-spoonful, his cheeks bulging.

SIXTEEN

Simon

We were in Liverpool by ten o'clock, and as our appointment was not until eleven, we spent an hour wandering around the Anglican Cathedral, just a short distance from the Clinic. It was a misty morning and at first sight the cathedral seemed to be floating in mid-air. It was so huge you could see it from almost anywhere in the city, Philip said.

He told us the city had held a competition and the winning design had come from a 22-year-old trainee architect, whose only previous design had been a pipe rack. Wow! I thought. Only 9 years older than me!

'What's a pipe rack?' asked Lissie 'How big is it?'

'It holds pipes for smoking tobacco,' said Philip, 'and it would probably be pretty small – small enough to stand on a desk, say.'

The cathedral, inside and out, was pretty impressive, but I was more impressed when I learned that its architect had also designed the red telephone boxes which you could find all over the country, and even in Malta where Mum had taken me for a holiday one year.

Then Mum was looking at her watch. 'It's time,' she said.

I looked at Ryan. He had been quite cheerful while we wandered around, but now he hung back and his face tightened up. Mum put out a hand to him.

'It's alright,' she said. 'Whatever the result, nothing will change. You're one of us now.'

'Yes!' said Lissie, and she flung her arms round him.

In the DNA Clinic Mum handed over the photographs of herself, Ryan and me, and the other documents that were needed, including a copy of the birth certificate for Ryan, which she had ordered online.

'But it's a fake,' I heard her say quietly. 'And that's why we need the tests, so that it can be corrected.'

Ryan was looking really pale now, and Lissie moved closer and held his hand. I was sitting on his other side and I didn't know what to do. 'It's going to be alright,' I said, but what did I know? Whatever the result, Ryan was likely to be upset.

The tests were just like I'd seen on television. Someone stuck something like a cotton bud in my mouth and rubbed it up and down, up and down, against my cheek. That seemed to go on forever, but later they told me it was sixty seconds, which was still much longer than in the films. I supposed in films there wasn't time to do it properly. After they'd taken it out they waved it about ('To dry it,' they said), and then did a second test, before sealing both sticks in an envelope.

So it took a while to do all three of us and put everything together, and then they said we'd have to wait several days for the results.

'I think I'd probably have dribbled if I had to keep my mouth open that long,' said Lissie as we left.

The sun was shining now, and we ate lunch at a pavement cafe near the cathedral. Mum and Philip treated themselves to a cocktail, even though it was the middle of the day. I think they were relieved that the tests were over.

'So, are we going shopping for my present next?' Lissie asked Philip.

He sighed. 'I suppose so. No rest until we do,' he said, but he was smiling. 'Actually, seeing you're bound to want to try on lots of clothes, I think Mum will take you, and we'll meet up later.' He turned to me and Ryan.

'You boys can come with me. I've an errand to do.'

After we'd dropped Mum and Lissie at the big shopping centre near the Pier Head and parked the car, we walked back in the direction of the cathedral.

'There's a shop along here I need to call at,' he said. We walked a little further and then he stopped. 'This is it,' he said.

It was a cycle shop.

'You're going to need transport,' he said to Ryan. 'I've picked out a bike for you.'

Ryan's mouth fell open. He tried to speak, but no words came out.

'Come and try it,' said Philip.

And then we were inside the shop and he was

leading us towards a bike in the far corner. 'This is it. Like it?'

Ryan stared at the bike, speechless. I think he was in shock.

'What if – what if - ?' he started at last, but Philip interrupted him.

'Whatever. It's yours. Try it. If it's OK, it will be delivered tomorrow.'

I sneaked a glance at Ryan, and he didn't disappoint me. His eyes had reddened and he was blinking hard. But I could understand how much this meant to him.

Ryan

On the way home Lissie sat between him and Simon. She chattered non-stop about some fabulous new outfit Caroline had bought her, and the other birthday presents that Caroline had chosen and had wrapped while Lissie was under strict orders to stay in the store cafe and drink a milk shake.

Ryan was glad he wasn't expected to say anything. He was still dazed. A bike! A brilliant one, too!

Everything that had happened, everything he was given, was binding him more tightly to this new family, and moving him further and further away from his Mum. Half of him still hoped the DNA test would prove he was not related. The other half . . .

But the bike! It was just like Simon's, and it must have cost a lot of money. They'd be able to ride to the new school together, Simon had said. Him and Simon and Lissie. He hadn't had a bike since the secondhand one his Mum had bought him when he was eight and which he'd had to leave behind when they left Cornwall. Joe had been too mean to buy him one, and his Mum had changed. She didn't want him out on the streets, she had said, and school was just five minutes' walk away, so there was no need for a bike. It was only now that he realised why she had wanted to keep him close.

His thoughts made him feel uncomfortable. Perhaps Joe had been telling the truth. Perhaps his Mum *had* hidden him when he was born, and then run away with him to Cornwall. But she had loved him. And he had loved her. And if anyone said bad things about her, he would – he would -

He felt Simon looking at him, heard him sigh, and he tried his hardest to stop the tears from falling. Lissie had stopped talking at last, and he felt her soft hand closing around his. A moment later she pulled out her phone, chose some music on Spotify, and began to sing along. '*Are you ready, are you ready for this? Are you hanging on the edge of your seat?*' Simon joined in, and the pair began to bounce.

It was irresistible. Ryan had to join in. The singing got louder, the bouncing got higher, and Ryan felt all his tension melting away.

'Hey, you three!' shouted Philip. 'I'm trying to get us home. Stop rocking the car!'

But none of them heard him, and by the time they reached the farm Ryan's tears had dried and he was feeling almost happy.

As they turned the last bend to the house Simon shouted out.

'It's Aunt Deborah! She's come early!'

A huge motorhome was blocking the drive. Philip stopped the car behind it and everyone piled out. Simon and Lissie ran forward and banged on its door.

'Aunt Deborah! Aunt Deborah!'

A sleepy eyed figure opened the door and stepped down. 'No need to shout. I was just having a light doze. But come and give me a hug, all of you.'

Ryan hung back and watched. Aunt Deborah was a giant of a woman. Almost six foot tall and heavily built, she was able to gather Simon and Lissie to her in one embrace. She glanced over their heads and gave him a huge, scarlet-lipped smile.

'Aunt Deborah!' said Caroline. 'We weren't expecting you until the weekend, but it's lovely to see you.'

Aunt Deborah released Simon and Lissie and raised her arms in a dramatic gesture. 'I've burned my boats! I've taken early retirement. I'm a free woman!'

'Oh, wow!' said Simon. 'Does that mean you're coming to live with us?'

She shook her head regretfully. 'I can't do that. But I can stay for a few days, if your Mum and Philip will have me.'

'Of course we will,' said Philip. 'For as long as you want. You're always welcome.'

'Thank you, darling!'

She marched towards the house, her colourful, multi-layered clothes lifting and floating around her at each step. At the front door she turned. 'Which of you is Ryan?'

There was nowhere to hide. Slowly he raised his

hand.

'Well, come along, young man. You and I need to have a chat!'

Simon

Poor Ryan! He had looked terrified, but no one could stay frightened of Aunt Deborah for long.

I followed Mum into the kitchen. She was taking a jug of home made lemonade out of the fridge and tipping some of Lissie's favourite peanut butter cookies on to a plate.

'I wonder if Aunt Deborah had any lunch. Go and ask her, will you, Simon.'

'She's talking to Ryan.'

'That's alright. She won't mind.'

And Ryan might be relieved, I thought, but when I went into the sitting room they were sitting together quite happily.

Aunt Deborah beamed at me. 'Pleased to have a new brother?'

'Yes,' I said. *When he's not crying,* I added to myself. 'Mum wants to know if you'd like lunch.'

'No, dear. I had a snack in the van.' She nodded at Ryan. 'We'll be with you soon, won't we, Ryan?'

I glanced at him, prepared to rescue him if necessary, but he didn't look too apprehensive. 'OK. See you later.'

Ryan

Aunt Deborah leaned forward. 'Now then, I want to

hear all about your Mum.'

'She wasn't wicked,' Ryan hurried to say.

'Has anyone said she was?'

'No, but they will, once they find out what – what she did.'

'Does Caroline think she was wicked? Philip? Lissie? Simon?'

'I don't think so.'

'So, tell me about her. Maggie? Was that her name? Tell me what she looked like. What she enjoyed – did she like books? Music? Dancing? Cooking? What did you and she talk about?'

Once started, it was hard for Ryan to stop. Since her death, and since Joe had confessed her crime, there had been no one he could share his memories with. It was as if she had been buried twice over.

But Aunt Deborah listened and asked questions, even laughed when he described the time in Cornwall when she had sneaked him into the hotel and up to the bedrooms where she cleaned and tidied and remade beds. How she had let him gorge on the chocolates that were laid on pillows, and how she had sneaked him out again in her trolley.

'She must have been a lot of fun,' said Aunt Deborah.

'She was. Before she met Joe.'

'You can talk to Caroline about her, you know. Caroline understands, and she doesn't want to destroy your memories. She just wants to love you and she hopes you'll love her – and the rest of the family. She doesn't expect you to wipe out thirteen years of your life.' Aunt Deborah glanced at her watch. 'Dear me – I think we may have missed all the cookies!'

At the door she turned. 'You know, Caroline couldn't have coped. Her father threw her out and she would have been forced to give you up – and that means both of you because she could never have chosen between you, it would have broken her heart. But now you're here, Ryan. This is the second stage of your life, and if Maggie's watching over you, she will want you to enjoy it, won't she?'

SEVENTEEN

Simon

The slamming of doors and the thud of footsteps down the stairs woke me before six o'clock. And then footsteps racing back up the stairs and my door crashing open.

'It's my birthday!' said Lissie.

'We know,' I groaned. 'Let me sleep.'

'No! What have you bought me?'

'I told you. Nothing.'

'I don't believe you. Where've you hidden it?' She had started pulling open drawers and was about to open my wardrobe. Her portrait was well wrapped and concealed by my clothes, but once she started rummaging she was sure to find it.

'No!' I sprang out of bed, catching my foot in the duvet and crashing to the floor. It hurt, but at least it distracted her.

'Aren't you even going to wish me Happy Birthday?'

'Happy Birthday. Many Happy Returns. Have a good day! Now go away.'

'OK. I'll go and wake Ryan.'

'Do that.'

By the time I'd had my shower and dressed, she was

downstairs, pestering Mum in the kitchen.

I knocked on Ryan's door.

'Go away!'

'It's me. Can I come in?' I opened his door. 'I should have warned you. She can be quite pushy when she's excited.'

'Well, she didn't find anything.'

He was sitting up in bed, eyes drooping and back hunched. 'I didn't finish until three hours ago. The birds had started singing before I got to sleep!'

'Wow! But you're pleased with it? Do you need any wrapping paper?'

'It's OK, I think. And Caroline gave me some paper last night.' He looked up, and there was that half smile again. 'The sketchbook and stuff – I really appreciate it.'

Downstairs Lissie was nagging Mum and Philip.

'I won't be able to eat a thing until I've had my presents,' she said.

'That's all right,' said Mum. 'You can make up for it at lunchtime.'

Aunt Deborah helped herself to porridge and poured a liberal amount of syrup on top. 'Patience, Lissie. There's an old proverb, "All good things come to those who wait". At least until breakfast is finished.'

Lissie watched us like a hawk after that, and the moment the last plate was scraped clean, the last cup emptied, she was on her feet.

Mum laughed. 'OK, we give in!'

But at that moment the front door letterbox clattered and Lissie was away. We waited, but she didn't come back. Aunt Deborah stood up. 'I'll go,' she said. She was back in a moment with Lissie clutching a handful of cards and torn envelopes.

'Nothing?' said Philip quietly. Lissie shook her head.

Mum stood up. 'Well then, time for all our presents. Who's going to start? Aunt Deborah?'

'Something to keep you out of mischief for at least half a day,' said Aunt Deborah.

'Oh, wow!' said Lissie as she opened the brightly wrapped package. 'What is it?'

'It's a wall collage kit for teens. I think there are about a hundred images in there, which should be enough to cover a whole wall of your room. Oh, and there's another present – I forgot to bring it down. I'll fetch it after breakfast.'

Mum and Philip were next. The new dress and shoes that Lissie would wear for her party, a new smart phone and a silver locket on a chain.

And then it was my turn. The portrait was quite large, especially now that it was framed. I ran upstairs and rescued it from the back of my wardrobe.

I watched as Lissie unwrapped it. She was quiet for several minutes as she stared at it, and then she looked up.

'Oh, Simon. It's beautiful.' Her fingers ran gently over the surface. 'Look at Petronella's feathers – and her little face!'

'I think it's pretty good of you too,' I joked.

'Yes. You've made me look quite pretty.'

'You are pretty,' said Ryan, and blushed as we all looked at him. I think it was the first thing he'd said since he came down for breakfast.

'It's wonderful,' said Aunt Deborah. 'You've

certainly inherited -' And then she stopped.

'Ryan,' said Mum. 'You're next.'

He looked nervous as he passed his present to Lissie, and I think he might have stopped breathing as she unwrapped it.

She stared down at the title on the cover of the sketchbook. 'Lissie and Sidney.' She looked up. 'Sidney? What -?'

'Open it,' he whispered.

We all watched as she slowly turned the pages. At last she looked up, her eyes shining.

'It's all about me – and Sidney, *our* Sidney. Oh my God, it's – it's me flying through the air on Sidney's back – and meeting other kids flying on the back of their pets – ponies, cats and – look, there's a flamingo – and strange places, and – oh, Ryan, it's magic! It's amazing!' She turned to Philip. 'It's a Manga book, and it's all about me, and Ryan's done it all himself!'

And she was up, and round the other side of the table, and hugging Ryan to death.

We all got a hug, but Ryan was the star of the morning.

But then Mum and Philip were on their feet again.

'We do have an extra present for you,' said Philip. 'If you'll all sit down again, we'll bring it in.'

'Do *you* know what it is, Simon?' asked Lissie when they had gone, closing the door behind them.

'No idea.'

Mum and Philip returned with a large box. We all watched as Lissie unpicked the rope that held it closed.

'Oh,' she breathed as she pulled open the top and reached down into the box. 'Oh!'

'Now you're going to be home from school every night, you'll be able to look after him,' said Mum.

The puppy was a ball of golden fuzz, tiny and wriggly, and already it was washing Lissie's face in a frenzy. That beat even Ryan's Manga book!

Aunt Deborah's other gift was a big, soft, cushiony dog bed. Lissie placed the puppy gently in it.

'What will you call him?' Aunt Deborah asked.

'Biscuit' Lissie whispered.

Philip smiled. 'She's been pestering me for at least a year. Name, breed, colour, all picked out!'

Later in the morning the doorbell rang. Mum answered it and came back carrying a parcel.

'For you, Lissie. From New York.'

Lissie replaced Biscuit carefully in his bed and took the parcel. She took a long time unwrapping it, as if she was scared of what might be inside, but at last the string and tape and paper were set aside, and a smaller, fancy box was opened.

'Come on, Lissie, what is it?' asked Philip.

'I think it's a wig,' she said softly. She lifted it out and let it dangle, long and wavy and golden. She looked as if she was about to cry, and then she jumped to her feet and rushed out of the room.

'Should I follow her?' asked Aunt Deborah.

'No,' said Mum. 'Let her be. She's bound to feel emotional. It's a long time since her mother's been in touch.'

But half an hour later Lissie came down. She had changed into the new clothes Mum had bought her, she was wearing the wig, and she must have borrowed a lipstick and some eye makeup from Mum's room.

She looked like a stranger, until she grinned, and we all laughed. Except for Philip. He had turned away, and I guessed he was thinking about Lissie's mother.

Ryan

He had been allowed to cuddle Biscuit before lunch, but only for ten minutes, because everyone else wanted a cuddle. He thought how lucky Lissie was to have so many gifts, to have so many people who loved her and to have a birthday party to look forward to in the afternoon.

He had never had a birthday party. In Cornwall his Mum was working as many days as she was allowed. They never had much money, and in any case, their apartment – two rooms over a shoe shop – was too small. The house in Liverpool had a little more space, but then his Mum hadn't wanted to meet other people. At the time he hadn't thought it strange, but looking back he guessed she had been scared. Scared of exactly what had now happened. That he might one day meet his look-alike. The baby she had left behind with Caroline.

The results of the DNA tests would be arriving any day now, and he could no longer pretend to himself that they would prove he and Simon were unrelated.

Aunt Deborah was watching him. 'I'm going to move my van before lunch,' she said. 'Want to look over it?'

He sat beside her as she started it up and drove it into the big yard behind the house.

'Now then,' she said. 'Let me show you how someone as big as me can live in quite a small space!'

He watched with fascination as she showed him

how the driver and passenger seats could swivel to form part of the seating arrangement, slid open half a dozen cupboards, lifted bench cushions to show the storage underneath, pointed out the refrigerator, the swing-out television, the sink with lift-up taps, and finally the bedroom with its two single beds, and the shower and toilet at the rear.

'Wow!' was all he could say. 'Wow!'

'Maybe one day you and I could take a little trip,' she said. 'Simon's been several times, and Lissie once.'

'I'd love that,' he said.

Aunt Deborah glanced at her watch. 'We'd better not be late for lunch. Caroline's going to be busy afterwards. She's got a very ambitious birthday tea planned. Your friends are coming, aren't they?'

'Melanie and Jasmine, yes.'

'And they're staying for a sleep-over, I hear.'

He hadn't known that. But he was pleased.

Simon

Lunch was bacon sandwiches, with fruit to follow, and I could see Ryan had got his appetite back. He looked relaxed and quite cheerful. Good old Aunt Deborah! I wished she could come and live with us permanently. I missed her.

'No chores for Lissie today,' said Mum when we'd finished, 'but you boys can load up the dishwasher and clear the table for me. Lissie, you can take Biscuit outside for a little walk. He's supposed to be house trained, but we don't want to take risks, do we? Especially today!'

Lissie had replaced her new shiny shoes with

trainers, and the wig was back in its box. The eye makeup and lipstick had disappeared too, and I saw Philip smile and give her a hug. I don't think he'd liked seeing her transformation this morning. I'd never seen a photograph of her mother but I wondered if Lisssie had looked too much like her.

In the kitchen Ryan was quite talkative. I could see he'd really taken to Aunt Deborah, and he'd loved the motor home.

'She said she'd take me on a trip sometime,' he said.

'You'll enjoy that. I've been lots of times,' I said, 'although not since Mum and I moved here'.

He looked at me. 'You don't really like the farm, do you?'

I shrugged. 'It's OK. It's just been a bit lonely, no other kids my age around, and my school too far away to meet anyone in the holidays. And I think Philip hoped I'd want to be a farmer.'

'And you don't want that?'

'I'm going to be an artist,' I said. 'Like my father.'

Ryan put the last few plates in the dishwasher and closed the door.

'What do you know about him?' he asked.

'Not much. Mum doesn't like to talk about him. I know he was eighteen, and very clever. And he was a really good artist. He'd had stuff in exhibitions, here in Liverpool. He and Mum were both hoping to go to University, but after she got pregnant – Anyway, he didn't want me, and he didn't want to stick around, so . . .'

'And you've never met him? He's never got in touch?'

'No. Mum would have said. But at least he gave me

something. The genes. And you've got them too. That Manga comic – it was brilliant!'

Ryan flushed. 'Thanks.'

We hadn't talked about the visit to the DNA clinic, but I had to say it. 'I really do hope the tests show we're twins, Ryan, and I hope you do too.'

I waited. He didn't say anything, but after a long minute he nodded, and smiled.

EIGHTEEN

Simon

Melanie and Jasmine arrived soon after lunch, and the three girls disappeared up to Lissie's bedroom. Immediately the screaming and giggling started, and then the thumps. I think they were jumping off the bed on to the floor. The dining room, where Ryan and I were helping Mum decorate the table for the birthday tea, was immediately below, and I'm sure I saw some flecks of plaster fall from the ceiling on to a bowl of salad. Mum rolled her eyes. 'Good job I covered it with clingfilm,' she said.

Later, after the girls had been introduced to Biscuit, Aunt Deborah led us out into the barn, where there were hay bales to sit on and Philip had draped strings of fairy lights from wall to wall.

'Oh, Lissie,' Jasmine sighed. 'You're so lucky! I'd love to live here.'

'Me too,' said Melanie. 'What about you, Ryan? Do you like the farm? Would you like to be a farmer?'

'Wouldn't mind,' he said.

It seemed I was the odd one out. But then I thought about it and realised that my own feelings had been changing. Now Ryan was here, and now Lissie and I were getting on better, and we'd all be going to a local day school, life wasn't so bad. I'd stopped thinking of

Philip as the enemy and the farm as a prison. I'd even milked a cow, and I might be willing to do it again, although there was no way I'd want to make a career of it.

Aunt Deborah delved into the big handbag she carried everywhere and produced a box of cards.

'Time for a game,' she said.

'Not charades! Aunt Deborah teaches drama,' I told the others.

'No, not charades. Something more fun. It's about characters, something I devised for my students. Each of you picks a card - there are lots of suggestions - and then you have to pretend you're the character on it. No speaking, no music, it must all be done with mime.'

'Sounds hard,' Lissie moaned.

'But fun,' said Aunt Deborah. 'So, pick a card, everybody!'

I'd played this game back in London at my last party there. At least it was one up on charades. Reluctantly I picked a card.

'Now, who's going to go first?'

Jasmine frowned at her card. 'What's an ornithologist?'

'Someone who studies birds.'

Jasmine still looked puzzled. 'Does it matter what kind of birds? I mean – would you have to pretend you're up a tree, or in the jungle, or a desert?' she asked.

Aunt Deboragh laughed. 'Well, it could certainly add something to your mime, but perhaps you'd better pick another card, now we all know what that one is!'

Mine was a shortsighted old woman searching for

her glasses, finding and putting on someone else's with the wrong prescription. Easy, I thought, and of course everyone guessed it. Lissie's was a baby in a high chair, trying to peel and eat a banana. Melanie's was quite clever. She had to mime a teacher writing something on a whiteboard. What was she writing? I was the only one who guessed it was an algebraic equation. Jasmine was excited by her second card. 'Ooh, can I borrow your wig, Lissie?' 'No props,' Aunt Deborah reminded her, but we all guessed quite quickly that Jasmine was a female pop singer.

When it came to Ryan, his smile disappeared after he'd picked his card. He stared at it for a long time and I thought he was going to refuse, but then he stood up and moved slowly towards an imaginary counter, picked up an imaginary glass and carried it carefully back to one of the hay bales. He sat down and stared at the glass. His posture changed. His shoulders hunched. His neck seemed to sink into them. His face changed too. His eyes narrowed. His mouth tightened. His chin jutted. He frowned and glared around him. He picked up the imaginary glass and pretended to drink, all in one go, whatever was in it, before slamming it down, standing up and pretending to shove his way out through a crowd. And then he was gone. Out of the barn and out of sight. We waited but he didn't come back.

'What was on his card?' asked Lissie.

'I don't know,' said Aunt Deborah.

'He was pretending to be Joe,' whispered Melanie.

'Oh dear,' said Aunt Deborah. 'There was a card for a drunken man. How unfortunate that Ryan, of all of us, should pick it.' She sighed. 'Perhaps that game wasn't a good idea.'

'I'll go and find him,' said Melanie.

'No, I'll go,' I said. I had no idea where to search, or what to say when I found him but watching Ryan mime so vividly Joe's anger and hatred I'd felt ashamed of all the times I'd been impatient, all the times Ryan's tears had irritated me. My own grumbles and complaints about leaving London, my school, my mates, seemed pretty trivial in comparison.

Ryan

He stood by the fence and stared at Sidney. Sidney stared back at him. Over the past week Ryan had spent quite a lot of time with the bull, sketching, taking photographs, ready to translate them into the magical animal who would carry Lissie on his back across the heavens.

He wished he hadn't picked that card. He knew he'd upset the girls, perhaps even Simon, and he'd embarrassed Aunt Deborah. But he had been enjoying himself, and then suddenly he was plunged back into a sea of dark memories. Joe's drunkenness and growing violence. Mum, disappearing a little bit more each day as her illness took over.

Mum. Mother. He didn't even know what to call her now. Mutti? No, he'd feel silly calling her that. And he couldn't call her just by her name, Maggie. That would feel as if he was disowning her. But . . . MaggieMum? He tried it a few times, feeling it strange on his tongue, but somehow right. She would always be Maggie, and she would always be his Mum. So . . . MaggieMum.

He walked on to the field fencing in Philip's sheep.

There were so many of them. He tried to count them but each time he thought he was reaching a total they surged and regrouped. He wondered how Philip managed them, all on his own. And then there were the cows, only a dozen or so, but more work. Perhaps he would offer to help. He would enjoy it. It would be a distraction and Philip would be grateful..

Of course, whatever Caroline said, if the DNA test showed she was not his mother, could he really expect her and Philip to keep him? Forever? What then? The thought of leaving, of being on his own again, brought new tears to his eyes.

'Ryan?' He heard Simon's voice behind him.

'Are you coming back? Aunt Deborah's sorry about that card.'

'Not her fault.'

'But she did think your acting was brilliant. Maybe that's what you'll decide to do when you leave school? If so, she could help you, she knows all sorts of people in theatres, films, too.'

'I wasn't really acting. Just remembering.' He wished Simon hadn't come.

There was silence behind him, apart from the rustle of leaves as a summer breeze came to life, the bleating of sheep in their field, and a deep rumble from Sidney. He didn't turn. He could feel the tears on his cheeks, still wet, and he pictured Simon rolling his eyes when he saw them. He couldn't blame him. Crying. It was such a cissy thing to do. Surreptitiously he rubbed his knuckles against them. He felt Simon's hand touch his shoulder.

'Ryan. I'm really sorry. I'd no idea – I hadn't realised how bad it had been for you. I know you haven't wanted to talk, but, well, anytime you decide to . . .'

The tears had dried. 'Thanks,' he said. He would have said more but the lump in his throat was huge.

'Coming back, then?' asked Simon.

Ryan nodded and turned. Simon slung an arm around his shoulders and the two boys walked back together.

Simon

Aunt Deborah had put her cards away and had been joined in the barn by Mum and Philip.

'Sorry,' Ryan mumbled.

'Nothing to be sorry for,' said Aunt Deborah. 'We're just waiting for the girls. We're going to have a fashion parade.'

'Does that mean Ryan and I can clear off?' I asked.

'Oh no! You're part of the audience, with me, your Mum and Philip.'

'You'll have to count me out,' said Philip. 'I need to move the sheep into a new field before tea. Actually, I could do with some help. You boys interested?'

'Yes, please,' said Ryan.

'Simon?'

I wanted to refuse but I hesitated too long. And actually, once we started I quite enjoyed it, especially running after the bolshie sheep who had no inclination to move house and gave us quite a chase.

When we returned, we met the girls, Melanie and Jasmine laden with piles of clothes, Lissie carrying her wig and the box of cosmetics Jasmine had bought her. They beat us into the house and disappeared up to Lissie's bedroom again. More thumps and bangs and screams. Ryan and I glanced at each other and smiled.

'I'm going to have a shower,' said Philip. 'You boys should clean up, too.'

'Actually, I was hoping for someone to help carry things into the dining room,' said Mum. 'Aunt Deborah's having a little lie-down. The girls have exhausted her.'

'I'll help,' said Ryan.

'Me too!'

'OK, but a quick shower first, I think. You're looking far to grubby to handle food.'

Nobody ever starved when Mum was around, and we all wondered how she kept so slim when she ate as much as any of us. By the time we finished, the dining table was groaning under the weight of all the dishes she had prepared.

The cake was missing. I knew she'd hidden it away, to be brought out after we'd cleared the table of everything else. I hadn't seen it but I knew it would be pretty special. Meantime there were hot sausages on sticks, mini burgers and quiches, pizzas, ham rolls and salad (nobody ate the salad). Afterwards there were marshmallow and melon kebabs, little fruit pies and crunchy chocolate slices.

I think we were all a bit greedy, and Philip suggested we wait a while before bringing in the cake.

'But not too long,' said Lissie, glancing at the clock and then at Melanie and Jasmine. 'What time do you have to go home?'

Melanie looked at Mum.

'They're not going home,' said Mum. 'We've arranged a sleepover.'

'Oh! Wow! Wow! Wow!' Lissie left the table and flung her arms around Mum. 'Thank you! This is the best birthday ever!'

I looked across at Ryan and rolled my eyes. There would be no sleep tonight!

Now, of course, Lissie wanted her cake cut immediately, so that the girls could retire upstairs. She also wanted Biscuit to take part in the sleepover, but Mum and Philip stood firm.

'He's not even fully housetrained yet,' said Philip.

When all of us had a piece of cake in front of us, Aunt Deborah stood up.

'Wait! I think we should all make a tiny speech before we take our first bite. I'll start.' She turned to Lissie.

'Lissie, my darling, my honorary niece – actually, my great-niece, but that makes me feel so old!. Thank you for welcoming me into your life. I have so enjoyed getting to know such a kind, loving young lady. Happy Birthday, darling!' She took a tiny bite out of her slice of cake and sat down.

Philip was next, but as he stood up Lissie cried 'Stop!' She rushed out of the room, to be back in seconds with the golden wig.

'Everybody has to wear it when they speak!'

I think Philip was embarrassed but he put it on, a little crookedly, as he told Lissie how much happiness she had brought him in the past twelve years.

After that, the wig passed from hand to hand as we all made our birthday speeches. It was looking a bit bedraggled by the time it reached Lissie again, and there were some biscuit crumbs and a smear of jelly caught in it. Lissie didn't seem bothered. I wondered if she was remembering who had bought it for her. Perhaps she no longer cared.

In an hour the sleepover was all organised, camp beds, duvets and pillows were moved into Lissie's room, and the girls came down to say goodnight. It was only seven thirty.

As the rest of us cleared the dining room, Mum raised her eyes to the ceiling. 'I hope that survives the onslaught!' she said.

At about nine o'clock Ryan pretended to yawn and said he was going to bed. I think Mum wanted to say something to him, but he was gone before she could begin.

Later, while she was making coffee, I looked for Philip. I found him in the sitting room, where he'd hung Lissie's portrait over the fireplace. He put an arm around my shoulders and drew me to him.

'Thanks for painting this, Simon,' he said. His eyes were moist. 'It's wonderful. You have a real talent. When Lissie's older she can hang this in her own house, and then later pass it on to her own children.'

I was as pleased by Simon's praise as by Lissie's delight earlier.

The noise from Lissie's room that night went on and on. My room was right next door. I thought the girls might break through the wall at any moment. At midnight I bundled up my duvet, pillows and a blanket and knocked on Ryan's door.

'What?' he whispered.

'I can't stand it any longer. Mind if I camp on your floor?'

He didn't answer, so I opened the door and crept in.

He lay, hands clasped behind his neck, a copy of Farmers Weekly tucked half under his pillow. I unrolled my bedding and lay down on the floor beside his bed.

We lay in silence for several minutes, then: 'Aunt Deborah was really worried about you,' I said. 'She couldn't have known, but she was really upset.'

'I shouldn't have done it. Should have asked for another card, like Jasmine.'

'Everybody understands.' I leaned up on my elbow. 'Joe's gone, Ryan. You'll never have to see him again.'

'But my Mum's gone too,' he whispered. 'I'll never see *her* again. And I won't even be able to talk about her because everyone will think she was wicked.'

'Mum and Simon and Aunt Deborah don't think that, and neither does Lissie, or Melanie – or me. And none of us is going to tell anyone. No one's going to know.' I waited, but he didn't say any more.

A moment later he switched off his lamp, but I lay awake for another hour. I'd made him a promise, but could I keep it? Could our family keep it? And were there others outside our family who knew? Melanie knew, but had she told her parents? And Jasmine? How much did *she* know?

NINETEEN

Simon

Two days later the DNA results arrived in the post.

'Is everyone ready?' asked Mum, when we were gathered in the kitchen. We all nodded.

She held the envelope for a long moment before opening it, and then she read the letter at least three or four times before she spoke. At last she looked up and her eyes fixed on Ryan. They were wet with tears, but she was smiling.

'Welcome to the family, Ryan,' she whispered. 'You're my son.'

His face had turned pale. He looked as if he too was going to cry. Philip, Lissie and I, we just stood there, waiting. None of us knew what to say.

'Can I have a hug?' asked Mum at last. 'Only if you want to, of course.'

Ryan hesitated. For what seemed forever. And then he moved forward, and Mum closed her arms around him.

I could hear Lissie sobbing, and Philip was clearing his throat, and my own throat felt a bit lumpy. I think I needed to get out and go for a mad bike ride or something, but there was no chance. Mum and Philip drew us all into a big family hug, and that was that.

I've got a brother, I told myself. A twin brother!

How crazy is that?

Later, after we had finished lunch, Aunt Deborah leaned back in her chair.

'Well,' she said. 'Time I went home, I think.'

'Oh no!' said Lissie. 'You've only been here a week, and you've got lots of time now you're retired.'

'But I have a new job to go to, darlings. You didn't think I'd be happy to sit at home and watch TV and crochet blanket squares, did you?'

'Tell us about it,' said Philip.

'I am to be consultant and drama coach for a local theatre group. Actually, I'll be a general dogsbody as well, but there'll be new projects, new friends. No more early rising. I shall be more of a night bird.'

'I hope they're going to pay you.'

'Ah, well, that does rather depend on whether their productions are successful and they sell enough tickets.'

'You'll miss the fete,' said Philip.

This was the annual charity event held on Philip's farm on the last Saturday before the schools' Autumn term. Lissie and I were looking forward to it.

'Yes. Such a shame. But I'll still come and visit you all whenever I can. In fact, I plan to be an absolute nuisance, turning up in my van at a moment's notice whenever I have a spare few days. Besides -' She turned and patted Ryan's head. 'I need to get to know this young man better.'

Ryan

He wished she wasn't leaving. He felt he could talk to her, explain his feelings and she would understand.

'Let's have a little walk round the farm,' she said,

after she'd packed all her bits and pieces into the van, including a dozen newly laid eggs and some fresh vegetables from Philip and Caroline, a quick sketch of her posing in Lissie's wig from Simon, and a long thank-you letter from Lissie. Ryan hadn't thought to give her anything. He felt embarrassed but she brushed his apology aside.

'The pleasure of meeting you is enough. So tell me, is everything good now? On a scale of 1 to 100, are you happy?'

Was he? She waited patiently while he considered.

'I still miss – *her*. But maybe 70 or 80,' he said at last. 'Most of the time.'

'Not bad. About level with the rest of us, then.' She burrowed in her handbag, took out a notepad and scribbled her number. 'Put that in your phone, and any time you want to talk, don't hesitate to call me. Any time,' she repeated. 'Sometimes it's easier with someone who's not too closely involved.'

Everyone was quiet after she'd gone. She had kept the talk going at lunchtime, but afterwards, after they'd all waved her goodbye, there was only one thing on all their minds and Ryan didn't feel ready to talk about that.

'Is there anything I can help you with?' he asked Philip.

'Well, you can help me clean out the chicken house, if you like, but you'll need your old clothes.'

'These are my only clothes, apart from the ones Simon lent me, but they were pretty new and I think they're in the wash.'

Philip looked shocked. 'Oh no, we hadn't thought! I'm sorry. Look, Caroline can take you shopping tomorrow – and you don't need to help today.'

'I'd like to.'

'OK, I'll lend you a boiler suit and some wellies. And you'll probably want a shower afterwards. It's a filthy job.'

Shooing out the chicks was the first task. Philip had scattered corn in the yard, and most of the hens vacated immediately and jostled each other to get their share, but there were others who refused to leave and glared defiantly. Philip just swept them up in pairs, one under each arm and threw them out the door. They didn't seem to mind, just sauntered around, pecking corn and acting as if that was what they'd intended anyway.

It was quite hard work, scraping up the droppings and brushing clean the perches and the dropping boards.

'Look out for any little piles of dust. They could be mites,' said Philip, and Ryan immediately felt itchy.

When they had finished and loaded all the droppings and old bedding into a wheelbarrow, Philip sprayed inside the house and put down fresh straw in the nest boxes. The chicks had cleared all the corn in the yard, and there was more jostling as they fought each other back into the house.

'You'll never teach hens to form an orderly queue. They prefer the continental way – every hen for herself,' said Philip. He glanced at Ryan. 'Did you enjoy that?'

Ryan thought for a moment. 'Yes. Actually, I did.'

Philip smiled. 'You and Simon, you're quite different really, aren't you? I would have expected identical twins to think alike, have the same interests, the same personality, but you two . . . Well, perhaps it's down to having different upbringings. I'm sure quite a few psychologists would like to get hold of you both and explore a bit deeper.'

'No!'

'Sorry, didn't mean to scare you. The last thing Caroline and I want is to expose you to that sort of thing!'

Simon

'Well, this morning went better than I expected,' said Mum. 'I thought Ryan would be devastated!'

'He likes you,' said Lissie. 'He likes all of us – even you, Simon,' she said, pulling a face at me. 'It's just because he doesn't want anyone to think badly about his real - I mean, his other Mum. Because that's like – like – upsetting.' She turned away, and I realised she was probably thinking about her own Mum.

Caroline glanced at her watch. 'I should phone Bill.'

'The police sergeant?' I asked. 'Why?'

'Well, to call off the search, I suppose. To tell him that Ryan is here.'

I looked out of the window. Ryan was still out in the yard with Philip.

'You can't do that,' I said. 'He doesn't want anyone to know.'

'But it's not right to let them go on searching.'

'I don't suppose they are. I expect Ryan's way down on their list.'

'Even so, I feel I should let him know, and that Social Services won't need to get involved, now we have proof Ryan's my son.'

I couldn't stop her. And it was a long chat. I couldn't

hear Bill's words, but it was clear he was very interested. I thought about my promise to Ryan and hoped I wasn't going to be proved wrong.

The next day Caroline drove Ryan, and Lissie and me into Liverpool. Our first call was to a school uniforms shop to be kitted out for Redmond House. Some of the stuff from our old schools could still be worn by Lissie and me, but Ryan didn't have anything, and we all needed new blazers (a dark red colour, like wine) and striped shirts and striped red ties. After that, we drove to the Liverpool One shopping centre and Mum bought jeans and other stuff for Ryan, who'd brought only what would fit into his rucksack when he ran away – and as far as we knew, his other clothes had been dumped by Joe Geoghegan before he disappeared.

There was so much Ryan needed that Lissie and I got bored, so we arranged to meet later in a nearby coffee shop. Philip had funded me again, so I treated Lissie to a giant meringue and a bottle of the really sickly cherry drink that she loved. Mum, although she herself made cookies several times a week, would have frowned at the sugar load. I had an iced fruit drink and a ham and cheese toastie.

We had nearly finished when I noticed a man at a nearby table looking over at me. He caught my eye then turned away, but a moment later he was staring again. I noticed he had an open newspaper beside him. Each time I looked up I caught him watching me, and suddenly I knew, I *knew* why he was staring.

'Come on, let's go,' I whispered to Lissie.

'But I haven't finished!'

'Come on!' I grabbed her arm. 'We need to buy a

newspaper.'

I sent Lissie into W H Smith's while I stood, my face to the wall, outside. As soon as she came out with the local paper I opened it. And there it was, on the front page. "Boy stolen at birth is reunited with his identical twin!" The photograph of Ryan, taken before he ran away from Joe, was displayed alongside it.

'Don't say anything to Mum or Ryan,' I told Lissie. 'Not yet.'

On the way home Ryan sat in the front. He had obviously enjoyed the day, and chatted happily with Mum, until she glanced in the driver's mirror at Lissie and me.

'You two are very quiet back there. Had a squabble?'

'Just tired,' I said quickly, and she went back to her chat with Ryan. But I wasn't tired. I was all strung up and worried about Ryan and my promise to him.

But most of all, I was angry with Mum. How could she have been so stupid? It was obvious that Bill had told his mates at the station, and that one of them, or perhaps Bill himself, had sold the story to the local Press. I'd seen so often on tv or in films what happened next. The Press would gather outside our home like a storm of locusts and we'd be trapped inside. There would probably be television cameras too. They might even be there now.

I glared at the back of Mum's head. This was her fault. But it was Ryan who'd be most hurt.

TWENTY

Simon

A call came through on my phone. It was Philip.

'The Press are here – a dozen or more! And BBC Television! There's a huge van blocking the drive. They're asking questions about Ryan. Do you know what this is about?'

'Yes,' I said. 'Tell you later.'

''Well, tell Mum to drive down the lane and park by the cottage. I'll sneak out the back way and meet you there.' His phone clicked off before I could answer him..

'Was that Philip?' asked Mum.

'Yes.' I didn't want to say more. Ryan would need some time before he faced the Press. 'Philip said the drive is blocked, so could you drive on and down the lane to the cottage. He's going to meet us there.' Perhaps we could hide Ryan in the cottage again. Just until nightfall, when I hoped the Press would have gone away.

I sneaked a look at him. He was smiling, chatting over his shoulder to Lissie. She was smiling too. I squeezed her hand and she nodded. I think she guessed what the blockage would be.

The cottage looked as abandoned as ever, its little garden waist high with weeds and grass. It seemed a long time since Ryan, Lissie and I had played house there with Melanie and Jasmine, yet it was only a few weeks.

'We should do something about this place,' said Mum. 'It would be useful for your friends to stay sometime. If we built an extension on the back we could even let it as a holiday cottage.'

None of us answered her. Ryan because he had hated his time there, Lissie and me because we knew why we were hiding there now.

A few minuts later Philip arrived. He moved straight to Ryan and put an arm around his shoulder.

'Ryan, I'm afraid the Press are here. I've refused to talk to them, but I can't get them to leave. It might be best if you hide out here until they're gone. I'm sorry, I don't know how they found out.'

'I do!' I said. 'It was Mum. She called Bill at the police station.'

Philip stared at her. 'Why did you do that?'

She looked shocked. 'I didn't think, I just wanted him to call off the search. I thought I could trust him!' She turned to Ryan. 'Ryan, I'm so sorry.'

Ryan turned his head away. I could see he was close to tears, and I couldn't blame him. I thought about the promise I'd made him. I'd never expected it would be my Mum who messed everything up.

'How long d'you think they'll stay?' she asked Philip.

He shrugged. 'All day, probably. If we're careful, I think we can creep back into the house and at least have some lunch.'

No one saw us, although one reporter had wandered round to the yard at the back. Fortunately a dozen or so chickens rushed upon him, obviously thinking he was bearing food, and he ran back to the front of the house. Philip had drawn all the downstairs blinds before he came out, so although the rooms were gloomy, we felt safe inside. Mum collected some cold stuff from the fridge and laid it out on the kitchen table, but none of us wanted to eat.

We sat round the table in the gloom created by the drawn blinds and stared at each other. Ryan looked too shocked even to cry.

'It's already in the Liverpool Echo,' I told them. I pulled out the screwed up newspaper from my jacket pocket and passed it to Mum.

'Please, what can I do to help?' said Mum, when she had read the report. She looked so pale, so upset. Part of me wanted to give her a hug, but I was still angry.

'I've no idea,' said Philip. His voice was cold. He was angry with Mum too. He opened a can of lager and drank it quickly. 'I'm going to phone the police,' he said. 'Find out what the punishment is when their own men sell stories to the Press! Ryan? You want to come with me?'

Ryan

Philip's expression was grim as he waited for the police station to pick up his call. 'Yes, Can I speak to Bill, please. He's a sergeant. I don't remember his surname.'

'Dixon,' said someone on the other end. 'I'll fetch him.'

'Don't worry, Ryan,' said Philip. 'We'll sort this.'

A few moments later Bill came on the line. Philip stood up and began to pace the floor. 'Philip Greenwood here. Lansdown Farm. My wife phoned you yesterday.'

'Yes, she did, and I had Ryan taken off the search list.'

'So, have you seen today's papers?' Philip asked. 'No, don't pretend ignorance! We're being bombarded by newspaper reporters, photographers, television – How much did they pay you for my boys' story?'

He had put his phone on loudspeaker, and Ryan could hear the police sergeant's gasp clearly. 'What? I know nothing of this!'

'My wife told you about the DNA connection. And now our family is front page news. I expect it's on the internet, too.'

'I promise you I have not spoken to anyone outside the station!'

'If not you, then one of your fellow officers or one of your staff. I expect you to find out. I want them punished and I want you to let me know what steps have been taken.' Philip's voice was icy. 'And I want the Press cleared from my property. Now. Otherwise, I'll be consulting my lawyer.'

Philip didn't wait for a reply. He turned to Ryan, and his voice softened. 'I'm sorry, Ryan. I'll do all I can to shield you, I promise.'

'But everyone will know about me. And about my Mum. And I'll be starting at the new school soon. They'll all know what she did.'

It was the first time Philip had hugged him, and it felt good. But not good enough to soothe his fears.

Simon

Bill and another policeman turned up half an hour later and cleared the Press off the farm. Bill was full of apologies and promised to find whoever was responsible for leaking Ryan's story. But no sooner had they gone then the phone started ringing again. It was BBC Television. They wanted to produce a programme special. Philip slammed down the phone.

We were able to open all the blinds and curtains and let the sunshine back into the house, but we could do nothing to help Ryan, who refused to eat anything at dinner – which showed how miserable he was, as he'd become practically a compulsive eater since half starving in the park.

We all went up to bed early, probably to lie sleepless, but none of us wanted to make conversation or play games or watch television. I was still angry with Mum and I was sure she'd noticed, although she hadn't said anything.

But next morning at breakfast Mum was brighter. She sat at the head of the table, erect, with a determined look on her face.

'I've had an idea,' she said. 'I'm going to contact the BBC and I'm going to tell my story. I shall talk about becoming pregnant at barely seventeen, and how scared I was. How my own mother had died, and I couldn't tell my father, who was very strict, and very religious. I shall tell how I found Maggie. How I had no idea I was going to have two babies, and was terrified when she told me.

'I didn't think I could cope even with one, because I would have to leave home. That's when I found out that Maggie couldn't have children and longed for a baby of her own.

'I will tell them I offered her one of my twins. Maggie

would be happy and I would be able to leave Liverpool to stay with my aunt with the one baby she was expecting me to bring.

'I'd say I had no idea I would ever see my other child again, but I knew it would have a happy loving upbringing with Maggie.'

'So -' Mum gazed at us all in turn. 'What do you think?'

'It's terrible!' said Philip. 'People would turn against you. They'd write nasty letters, make comments on the internet – you'd be ostracised. I won't allow it!'

'Better me than Ryan. And I think most people would understand that I was hardly more than a frightened child myself at the time, which was certainly true.' Mum stared at us all defiantly. 'Anyway, I'm going to do it, and you can't stop me! At least Ryan won't have to face criticism of Maggie.'

Philip turned to Ryan. 'What do *you* think?'

Ryan was looking very pale, apart from his eyes which were still red from crying. 'I don't know! I don't know! Don't ask me!'

'Philip, stop! You can't ask Ryan to decide. Anyway, I'm going to do it, whatever any of you say. It was my fault it got in the papers, I have to sort it out, and that's that!' And she got up and stormed out of the kitchen.

I followed her upstairs.

'Do you want me to come with you?'

'I expect they'll just do a video interview.'

'I think you're very brave.'

'You were angry with me. You needn't deny it, Simon – and I don't blame you. I was stupid, and it's up to me to make it right - and actually, I shan't care what people think or say. I've got my family. I've got my two boys.' She reached out a hand and stroked my cheek. 'You like him, don't you, Simon?'

I hesitated. 'I'm not sure he likes *me*.'

'He's had a hard time, I don't suppose the last few years

living with Joe Geoghegan were very good. And then Maggie dying. Give him time.'

An hour later the interview had been arranged. 'We'll use the desktop computer in Philip's office,' said Mum. 'And – er – they'd really like to meet the whole family.'

'No!' said Philip.

'No!' said Ryan.

'Ooh, yes!' said Lissie.

'Please,' said Mum. 'You won't have to say anything. You'll just have to smile – especially you, Ryan. And maybe you and Simon can sit close together and look happy.'

'Look like idiots, you mean!' I said.

Mum sighed. 'It won't be for long. Half an hour at the most, and then it will probably be edited down to ten minutes or even less. We just need to satisfy everyone that we're not newsworthy.'

'I'm going to change into my new dress!' said Lissie, and she rushed upstairs.

'Ryan and I are dressed alike. Should one of us change?' I asked Mum.

'I don't think it matters.'

Philip said nothing. I could see he hated the whole idea, and was still worried that Mum might become the butt of criticism. He would probably try to change her mind right up to interview time, but I knew how stubborn she could be.

Ryan

She had asked him to stay with her. When the others had gone, she led him over to the little sofa by the bedroom window.

'How do you feel about this, Ryan?'

'Nervous.'

'But are you happy with what I'm going to say?'

Yes? No? It was amazing that she was willing to do this for him. He wanted to say yes, but that felt mean. Wrong.

'I wish you didn't have to lie for me.'

'It won't bother me, Ryan, and if people criticise me, so what? Water off a duck's back, as they say. We're a close family, all the closer for having you in it, and that's what matters. Now – do I deserve a hug, or don't I?'

He moved forward into her arms. It felt good. He felt he should say something. What? He still wasn't sure what to call her. Mutti, as she'd suggested? He whispered it in his head, but he still couldn't bring himself to say it out loud.

Simon

We were all a little nervous during the interview. Most of the time Philip looked as if he was suffering from indigestion, but the rest of us, even Ryan, smiled like crazy. I think we probably fooled everyone. And Mum was magnificent. I hadn't known she could act so well. She switched so easily from today's happiness and contentment to the terror she had felt as a pregnant and very young girl, and back to the joy of finding her other child again. No one would have suspected there was a very different story behind the one she was telling. As I watched I realised it was from her that Ryan got his acting talent.

'All done, ' she said, when at last we were allowed to sign off. 'Nothing to worry about now.'

'I need a strong drink after that,' said Philip when it was over.

'I loved it,' said Lissie. 'That's what I want to be when I leave school. A television presenter!'

Ryan said nothing.

Mum squeezed his hand. 'It's all just local news. Here today and gone tomorrow. I don't suppose anyone will see it outside this area.'

But she was wrong.

TWENTY ONE

Ryan

Ryan woke early the next morning, but Caroline and Philip were already downstairs, tapping away on their laptops.

'The annual Fete is less than two weeks away,' said Philip. 'We're late starting. The exhibitors and the fairground people have booked their spaces, but there's still lots to do. Lissie's an old hand at it, but I'm hoping you and Simon will help.'

'What can I do?' Ryan asked.

'Would you like to take over the car parking? It's going to be in the field from which we've just moved the sheep. The signs are in the barn, and we need a few young people to direct drivers into lanes. Simon doesn't have any local friends yet, but maybe you could see if any of your school mates could help?'

'I could ask Melanie and Jasmine. I'm not sure about the boys. I wasn't – I wasn't really popular. I didn't – my Mum didn't really let me join in much -'

'I understand. Well, I expect three of you will be enough, if the girls are willing, but I can give you the phone number for a couple of my friend's sons, too. Meanwhile,' said Philip, 'I thought it would be good to have a new design for the posters and programme covers and I thought you and Simon could get together and work out something more exciting than the previous years. What do you think?'

'I'd love that!'

'Thought you would. I'll find some of the older covers, which I'm sure you two could improve on.'

Ryan couldn't wait. He took the stairs two at a time and rapped on Simon's door until a sleepy voice croaked, 'Enter'.

'Philip wants us to design the programme for the annual Fete! The two of us!'

'What? Right now?'

'You can have breakfast first. I'm not hungry.'

Simon sat up in bed, his eyes still slits. 'What time is it?'

'Six thirty.'

Simon groaned and lay down again.

'OK. I'll start without you.'

'No, you won't!'

Simon

After breakfast Philip took us into his office and rooted out some of the older programmes and posters.

'The Fete is in aid of the local children's hospital,' he said. 'I've been loaning them a couple of my fields for the past eight years but I've gradually got more and more involved. We've never had a really exciting poster or programme cover, so I phoned a friend there and told him I had a couple of bright young artists who'd like to take over, and he said Yes.'

He spread everything out on his desk. 'As you'll see, they're pretty dull. The information's OK, but there's nothing on the posters to make people feel they've got to be there. If you can create something more exciting between you, it might encourage even more visitors.'

'These are all black and white. Can we use colour?' asked Ryan.

'Yes, we can print the programmes off here, although the posters will have to go to a print shop. I'm still waiting for confirmation on some of the events and stallholders, but if you can produce something fairly quickly, say in a couple of days, I'd appreciate it.'

'We can do that,' I said quickly. I glanced at Ryan. He was smiling.

'Definitely,' he said.

Mum cleared the dining room table for us and we spread out the old posters and covers. Even if they had been in colour, they would have been pretty boring.

'If we go through the events that are listed, we might come up with something interesting,' I said.

There were all the usual things you find at fetes. Stalls selling ice cream and burgers, stalls selling books and bric-a-brac, a dog show, various competitions, pop groups, cake stalls and a hog roast, even a carousel. I wondered aloud how big that was, and how much space it would take up.

Lissie had joined us. 'It's full size and it's brilliant,' she said.

'And will it be here this year?' asked Ryan.

'Oh, definitely. It makes a lot of money for the owner, and half of it will go to the children's hospital.'

'That's it, then,' said Ryan. 'A carousel.'

'Can you find us some photos of it?' I asked Lissie.
'Easily.'

'So, are we just going to put a photograph on the front?' I asked Ryan.

'No, we'll draw it and colour it and pack it with children, all waving and laughing!' said Ryan. 'Or maybe just one section. One horse, one child.'

'Still waving and laughing, but maybe wearing bandages?' I joked.

'Wow' said Lissie. 'Good idea, but you'd better check it out with Dad and the hospital before you start!'

'I'll do a quick pencil sketch now,' said Ryan. And he did. It took him about four minutes.

I stared down at the prancing horse, the laughing girl on its back, her eyes sparkling at us, her long curly hair blowing in the breeze. I couldn't produce anything like that. I could paint a portrait, paint sheep and cows, paint landscapes, but however good they were, it was just copying. Ryan had all the imagination. Inside all his quietness, his gloominess, was this amazing talent, ready to spring out. As a manga comic, as this brilliant sketch that seemed to leap off the paper.

'You haven't given her a bandage,' I said quietly.

'Ah!' Quickly he rubbed out one of her arms and repositioned it, now wearing a sling.

'Fantastic! Let's show Dad,' said Lissie.

'No, I'll do it properly so it's accurate against a real carousel, and I'll colour it in.'

Within half an hour the sketch was finished and Ryan had even roughed in the words that would appear with it, and we took it in to show Philip and

Mum.

Philip looked at it for a long time. Ryan began to fidget and look nervous.

Then Philip looked up at him. 'It's wonderful. I'd no idea you had so much talent.'

Then he looked at me.

'Two artists in the family. And both brilliant.' He smiled, a little sadly. 'I don't think I'm going to make farmers out of either of you!'

'I'll be your farmer, Dad,' said Lissie. 'I love it!'

'Thank goodness – But I thought you wanted to be a television presenter?'

'I can combine both. I'll be a lady farmer, dressed in the latest fashions, and present a weekly programme about Life on Landsdown Farm.'

Mum came forward and gathered all three of us into a hug. 'That's the future settled, then!'

I should have been pleased for Ryan. I was, but I felt left out. What would be my contribution, apart from putting together the list of events and stallholders? Boring stuff.

But Ryan had other ideas.

'I'm not much good on computers. I never had one of my own. So I'm wondering - would it be possible to create a border for the poster, and then minimize it to use inside the programme? You know, the kind of things you might see at a Fete? Say, candy floss, balloons, flags, ice cream cornets, tents and stuff? Could you do that, Simon?'

I shrugged. 'Yeah, I suppose I could. Would be quite difficult, of course – the scale, everything minimized. You wouldn't get much detail. But – OK.'

Actually, it wouldn't be difficult at all, even Lissie

could have done it. Most time would be spent looking up suitable images. Shame Ryan had never had a computer, though. It seemed he hadn't had much of anything.

When I'd finished and we'd put it all together, we took it to show Philip.

'It's wonderful! You have so much talent, both of you. I'll forward it to the chief at the hospital, just to get his approval, and then we'll get everything printed. Nice work, boys!'

Ryan

It had been a good morning, and the glow from Philip's praise lasted all through lunch. His Mum - 'MaggieMum', as he had now trying to think of her – had always praised his talent. But where had it come from? Not from her, and even if the imaginary father she had conjured up for him had existed, it was unlikely that someone with real artistic skills would have chosen to become a sailor.

And then there was Simon. Both of them with the same talent. Those genes must have been passed down from their real father, the one Caroline never talked about. Wasn't Simon curious about him?Ryan longed to know more.

'Want to go for a ride?' he asked Simon when lunch was over. He had his own bike now. It still brought a flush of pleasure every time he thought about it.

'OK, why not?'

'Me too!' said Lissie.

Ryan was about to say No, but he'd noticed how often Simon shut her out. He knew what that felt like. It had happened so often at school, where the other boys had labelled him a Mummy's boy and a softie and left him out of their plans and games.

'OK, where shall we go?'

'Sefton Park,' said Lissie promptly. 'You can show me where you hid.'

'Not sure he'd want to be reminded,' said Simon.

'It's alright,' said Ryan. 'The woman in the cafe there gave me a huge bag of food that first day. I'd like to thank her.'

Simon laughed. 'She mistook me for you, when I was there with Melanie and the others. It'll be fun to show her both of us together!'

'OK, Sefton Park it is.'

It felt a little weird, going back there, but already time was smoothing over the memories. He'd been lucky, he told himself. If Simon hadn't seen his photograph in the paper, if Simon and Melanie hadn't met and talked that day, if Caroline and Philip hadn't been so kind, where would he be now?

The cafe was busy in the afternoon sunshine. Leaving Lissie outside to guard a table, he and Simon went inside to order. Yes, the same woman was behind the counter. Her mouth fell open when she saw the two of them.

'*You* – What ? Well, I'm – What's going on?'

'We're twins,' said Simon. 'We've been apart for a long time, but now we're together again.'

'Well, blow me!'

The queue behind them was beginning to grumble, so they ordered quickly.

'I wanted to thank you – for the food that day,' said Ryan, as the woman put bottles and cakes on the tray and took their money.

'Nearly gave me heart failure, you did! Thought I was seeing things,' she said, but she smiled. 'Well, good luck to you both!'

It was a hot sunny day and the terrace outside the cafe was packed with visitors. Lissie was struggling to keep at bay those who wanted to share her table or borrow a chair.

'You were a long time!' she accused them, but her glare disappeared when she saw the plate of cakes. 'Ooh! Can I have the chocolate doughnut?'

When they had finished eating and drinking, Simon leaned back in his chair.

'Come on then, Ryan, what is it? I can see you're bursting to tell us something.'

Could he trust them? 'You won't say anything to Caroline or Philip?'

'Depends what it is.'

'I'm good at keeping secrets.' said Lissie.

'OK. I want to find my real father. *Our* father,' he said to Simon.

'Why? Aren't we enough for you? Mum, and Philip and Lissie? Me?'

'I just want to know where – and what – I came from. So far I've had a mother who wasn't my mother, a father that she just made up out of her head, Joe who appeared out of nowhere and wasn't even my stepfather – I need to know more about my real family, And that has to include my real father, who nobody wants to talk about.'

'You want to meet him?' asked Lissie.

'Yes. No. I don't know. Aren't you curious about him, Simon?'

'I was. I'm not really bothered now. I'm happy just

to have Mum. And you should be, too.'

'But don't you want to know about our genes? We're both artists, pretty good ones, and that's not from Caroline. What sort of artist was our father?'

Simon shrugged. 'I've given up asking. Mum doesn't want to talk about him.'

'We could try to find him on the internet. You could show me what to do.'

Neither Simon nor Lissie looked happy.

'Caroline doesn't have to know,' said Ryan. 'Please!'

'If he's been successful, he'll probably be on Google. Maybe we can see some of his paintings, maybe a photograph of him, but that's enough. I'm not going to help you meet him. I'll tell Mum if you try.'

'OK,' said Ryan. But Lissie was frowning at him. She didn't look convinced.

TWENTY TWO

Simon

I tried Google first, and keyed in whatever details I had. I knew his name wasn't on my birth certificate, and Mum had never told me his surname. All I had was his first name, Oliver, when he was born - eight months earlier than Mum – the school he'd attended, and the city, Liverpool. All the information was thirteen, nearer fourteen years old.

We were in my room, Ryan, Lissie and me. Mum and Philip were downstairs, watching something on television. I felt mean. I knew Mum would hate it if she knew what we were doing. Twice I tried to put Ryan off, but he was determined. His eyes were bright and he was hardly breathing.

I was hoping to find lists of pupils but there weren't any. But then Lissie suggested I look for school photographs. Sometimes at her school they took photos if someone won a special prize or did something heroic that got into the papers, she said. OK, I said, let's try it. And we found him. A Sixth Form student, who had won First Prize in a painting competition run by one of the city's art galleries. The year was right, his age was right, and he was an Oliver. There could have been other Olivers in the school but were they prize winning artists? His surname was Daizley. It wasn't a surname I'd come across before. I tried it silently on myself. Daizley. *Simon* Daizley. It felt weird.

'What do we do now?' asked Ryan.

'We Google him. See if he took up art professionally.'

And there he was. Oliver Daizley, Portrait Painter. There was even an exhibition of his paintings taking place right now in Birmingham. Was that where he lived?

I keyed in to the exhibition, and the first thing we saw was a photograph of him. Oliver Daizley. Standing at an easel, a paintbrush in his hand. His left hand. So he was more like me than Ryan.

'Look! Look!' said Lissie. 'It *is* him. Look, you've all got the same nose, with the wonky bit on the end.'

'Thanks,' I said, and Ryan fingered his own nose.

We all stared at the photograph for ages. The screen kept blanking and I had to bring it back.

'Do you want to view the exhibition?' I asked. They both nodded. Actually, I wanted to see it too, but I didn't want to decide.

The portraits were good. Pretty brilliant, in fact. Was I as good as him? No. Not yet. But I intended to be. Better, if possible.

'What do we do now?' Ryan whispered.

'Nothing,' I said, and closed my laptop down.

Ryan

He couldn't sleep. Midnight passed. And then one o'clock. Two o'clock. At three o'clock he switched on his light and reached for his phone. Perhaps his father was on Facebook. His Mum had never let him have an account of his own but he had always had access to hers. He keyed in her password, and then started a search.

Yes!

There was not much personal stuff. It was used mainly to promote exhibitions and to attract new clients. There were photographs of his studio, huge, impressive, one with someone posing for a portrait, someone Ryan thought he recognised from television. There were lots of portraits, a handful of landscapes and townscapes, one of a yacht – Ryan wondered if it was Oliver Daizley's own. There were few personal photographs, no one that Ryan recognised, nothing under Likes. Nothing, Ryan thought, that taught him anything more about the man who could be – no, almost certainly, was - his father.

He closed his phone down and switched off his light.

An hour later he switched it on again. Found Facebook and clicked on Messenger.

'My name is Ryan. I think I'm your son. And I'm an artist, like you!'

He waited for a response. Nothing. Of course, it was four o'clock in the morning. Apart from himself, who would be awake at that time? He switched off his light and tried to sleep.

Simon

'What's wrong with Ryan?' asked Philip at breakfast. 'He's usually first at the table.'

I glanced at Lissie, she glanced at me.

'We were pretty late last night playing games,' I said.

Lissie stood up. 'I'll go and check him.'

'His light was still on, and he just mumbled something when I tried to wake him,' she said, when she returned. 'Shall I take something up to him?'

'No,' said Mum. 'Best leave him to sleep – although it's not like him to miss out on food!'

I guessed he had probably lain awake half the night thinking about Oliver Daizley. Our father. Even I had found it hard to sleep. I looked at Lissie and she looked at me. I think both of us felt guilty. I wanted to tell Mum what we'd been doing, but if nothing more happened, it was better she didn't know.

Ryan

He awoke to the sound of Philip's tractor. He looked at his watch. It was almost midday. He had missed the whole morning, missed breakfast, almost missed lunch.

He picked up his phone. He counted ten, his finger hovering over the buttons. Maybe he should wait until he'd had lunch. But no, he needed to know now. He clicked on Facebook.

There was no reply. Nothing.

Perhaps Oliver Daizley hadn't seen the message yet. Perhaps he also was sleeping late, or perhaps his phone wasn't charged, or perhaps he made it a rule not to look at Facebook or any other distractions until he'd finished whatever he'd been painting the previous day. There were any number of reasons why he hadn't replied.

So Ryan sent him another message.

He knew Simon and Lissie would be angry with him, but he pushed the knowledge away.

Downstairs Caroline was setting the kitchen table for lunch. She smiled. 'Afternoon, lazybones!'

'Sorry. Where is everybody?'

'Philip's harvesting wheat, and Lissie and Simon went out on their bikes. They should all be back in by one o'clock. You don't want breakfast, do you?'

He shook his head. He wondered what she would say if she knew what he'd done.

'I'll just go outside. Walk around a bit,' he mumbled.

He stood in the yard, watching the chickens feeding on their morning mash. When they saw him they rushed forward, hoping he might have something more exciting for them. He stood there, letting them peck at his ankles and his trainers.

When the others returned for lunch, he kept his eyes on his plate. He couldn't look at any of them.

Simon

I phoned Melanie. 'Has Ryan been in touch with you today?'

'No. Why?'

'I can't tell you now.'

'Want me to come round?'

I hesitated. 'Yes. OK, but maybe I'll meet you by the cottage. I don't want him to know I'm talking to you. Oh, and don't bring Jasmine. Not this time.'

'You sound very mysterious, Simon?'

'No. Just a bit worried.'

I spoke to Lissie after I'd finished the call.

'I'm sure Ryan's up to something. He won't look at me – at any of us. Can you keep him out of the way while I explain to Melanie? I think Ryan listens to her.'

'I'll try. But maybe we should tell Mum and Dad.'

'Not yet. Wait till Melanie's had a go at him.'

Ryan

Ryan checked his phone for the twentieth time. Although it showed that Oliver Daizley had now seen his messages, he still hadn't replied. Maybe he thought it was someone playing games, or wanting to get money from him. Ryan wondered if he should message him again. Was there any point?

He wandered round the house, unable to settle anywhere. Caroline appeared in the kitchen doorway, water dripping unnoticed from her yellow Marigold gloves.

'Is something wrong, Ryan?'

'No,' he said quickly. 'Nothing's wrong.'

He hovered in the barn, watching Philip as he stacked hay bales in his trailer to take out to the fields.

'Want to help? Philip asked. 'No thanks,' Ryan answered.

He wandered across the fields, watched by Sidney. The bull lumbered towards him as he drew closer.

'Morning, Sidney. What do *you* think I should do?'

But the bull had nothing to say.

And then suddenly Melanie was there.

'Simon called me. What's going on?' she asked.

'Nothing.'

'Yes there is. Tell me!'

So he told her.

'You sound quite proud of him,' she said, when he came to a stop, 'but he can't be a nice man, can he? He dumped your Mum – your *real* Mum – when she needed him, and he's not interested in *you*.'

'He's probably just too busy to answer my messages yet.'

'I bet he isn't. He just doesn't want to know. Accept it. You've got a lovely new family here, Ryan, you're so lucky. Think how upset Caroline will be if she finds out. Philip too. All of them.'

He turned away.

'What's more important?' Melanie said to his back. 'Your family – *this* family – or some selfish stranger who's never taken an interest in Caroline or you and Simon?'

'I just want to know more. We've got the same

artistic genes.'

'So what? I bet you and Simon between you have more of them and better ones than he has. Anyway, if he ever came here, I bet Philip would punch him, and then Philip would be in trouble! Forget him, Ryan.'

Sidney had lost interest in them both and was now just a brown shape against the far corner of his field.

'It's easy for you to give me advice, Melanie, tell me what to do. You've had the same Mum and Dad all your life. You know who they are, who *you* are, and you all love each other. You're lucky.'

'And you're not? How lucky is it to find a new family who love you and want to look after and protect you? How lucky is it to live here on this fantastic farm? Honestly, Ryan, you just don't know how lucky you are!'

She shook her head in disgust. 'I'm going home!'

He watched her as she stomped towards the house. And then she turned.

'By the way – Joe's back. My Dad saw him in the pub last night. Don't know where he's staying. Not at the house, that's already got new tenants in. But he's back. Maybe *he'll* look after you when you've lost *this* family!'

Joe! All the bad memories crowded back into Ryan's head. The summer in Cornwall when MaggieMum and Joe had first met. Joe had pretended to take an interest in Ryan, but even then, even at eight years old, Ryan had known Joe didn't really want him. And then, after they all moved to Liverpool, Joe had begun to pick on him, criticise him, but only when MaggieMum wasn't there.

It got worse. MaggieMum knew about it, but the

more she tried to console him, the worse Joe became, inventing little punishments, buying sweets and stuff for her but none for Ryan, refusing to pay for even a secondhand i-Pad or laptop to help with his homework. She knew, but she had no money of her own, and Ryan thought she had begun to feel a little scared of Joe. Too scared to protest.

And then she became ill. And then she died. And that's when Joe began to hit him.

And now Joe was back.

Why? What did he want?

TWENTY THREE

Simon

Ryan, Lissie and I milked *all the cows* this morning. Unbelievable. Six months ago, six weeks ago I couldn't have contemplated it. Lissie was in charge, of course. She'd lived on the farm all her life and knew exactly what to do. She did become quite bossy but Ryan and I, both of us thumb-fingered, didn't really mind.

I expected we'd have to do the milking tomorrow too, as Philip and Mum would be busy supervising the setting up of stalls and tents, and putting signboards and arrows in place to direct the visitors. Lots of tickets had been sold. 'Twice as many as last year,' said Philip, 'and that's down to you two artists and your amazing posters.'

Melanie and Jasmine had been with us almost constantly, and later in the morning Jake and Josh, sons of Philip's friend, came round for final instructions on car parking.

'Wow!' they said, when they saw Ryan and me. 'We watched your Mum's TV interview. How did it feel to find each other?'

'Great,' I said. 'Great,' Ryan echoed.

But not 100% great, I added to myself. I still felt

angry that Ryan had tried to contact our father, after all that Mum and Philip had done for him.

Mum fed us with burgers at lunchtime. All nine of us. She looked flushed and tired, but happy. I think she really enjoyed everything about farm life, and nothing seemed too much trouble for her. Looking around the table, I still felt like the odd one out, but only slightly now. Very slightly. And really, Ryan, although he was laughing and chatting away to the girls, was still the real odd one out. He was the one who was threatening to upset everyone by contacting our father.

Ryan

He had checked his phone again that morning. Still no reply. Perhaps he should have given more information about himself, but it was too late now, he decided. It was disappointing, but at least he had tried, and Simon might stop ignoring him if Ryan told him he had given up.

The two boys he'd just met, Jake and Josh, were good fun. He wondered if they might become his friends. At his old school his only friends had been girls. The boys had mocked and bullied him because he didn't join in with anything outside school, because he always had to go home straight away. They had called him names, ganged up around him in the playground and taken turns to knock him to the ground.

He had blamed everything on Joe, but he realised now the problem was more down to Maggie Mum. She had kept him so close to her, hardly letting him out of her sight outside school hours. He often thought she would have preferred to keep him home from school too, if she had been allowed. She had been so different before she met Joe, before they moved to Liverpool. She'd been fun and she'd allowed him to have fun, mixing with all the kids around, boys and girls.

Joe. Melanie had said he was back. Why? What did he want? Perhaps he was planning to come to the Fete, try again to get some money from Philip. Joe knew Philip had a big farm, was probably quite wealthy, and Joe was always short of money. Would he turn up at the Fete tomorrow? Ryan shivered. He wondered if he should warn Philip and Caroline, but what good would that do? They were going to be so busy, and he didn't want to spoil the day for them.

He could hear the clattering of dishes, the running of water, the throb of the dishwasher from the kitchen. He wandered in. Caroline was at the sink, her shoulders slumped now with tiredness.

'Can I do anything to help?' he asked her.

She turned and smiled. A big, loving smile. 'Thanks, Ryan, but there's no need. Go and have fun with the others.'

He hesitated. He wanted so much to tell her. About Joe. About Oliver Daizley. But how could he?

Simon

In the afternoon half a dozen of the stallholders arrived and began setting up, ready for the morning, but the big excitement for me and Ryan and Lissie was the arrival of the carousel. I hadn't realised it would be a full size fairground ride. I had expected one of those seen in town centres for small children.

We weren't allowed to help in the setting up, but everything else was on hold for us while we watched.

It was sundown before the owner and his mate finished. The carousel was enormous. It dwarfed everything else in the field.

'Aren't the horses beautiful?, whispered Lissie. Most of them were white, with brightly coloured saddles and reins. 'I like the ones with the scarlet saddles and the golden manes,' she said. 'I like the blue and gold,' said Ryan. There were a few black horses scattered amongst the others. 'I like that black one – the one with an orange mane and turquoise and orange saddle,' I said.

Then the carousel owner switched on all his lights - but not the music - and invited everyone to have a ride. Lissie rushed back for Biscuit and took him with her, hugging him tightly as she rode her scarlet and gold horse. It was magic. The horses moving up and down, in a circle of golden light, the only sound the whistling hum from above the canopy. Outside the circle of golden light, nothing but darkness.

Lissie had asked the owner what made the horses go up and down. He had shown us the crankshafts hidden above the canopy, one attached to each horse's pole, and how they turned, lifting and lowering the horses as they circled.

'That's useful to know,' said Lissie. 'It *is!*' she insisted as we laughed. 'I might need to mend machinery later, when I'm running the farm.'

'Well, good for you, Miss. What about you boys?'

'Oh, they wouldn't want to get their hands dirty,' said Lissie. 'They're artists.'

The next day we were woken at six thirty. 'No excuses, no grumbles,' said Mum. 'There are cows to milk, chickens to feed, and the rest of the stall holders will be arriving early to set up.'

Our helpers, Jake and Josh, Melanie and Jasmine, also arrived early, and after a hot drink and one of Mum's cookies, each of us was set to a task. There was a lot to do. We were all kept busy until the visitors started arriving at ten o'clock. Philip and I were on gate duty for the first hour, selling programmes and directing cars to the car park.

It was my first Fete – I don't think we had them where Mum and I had lived in London – and I was enjoying it. I was enjoying it all, I realised. The farm, the countryside, being with Philip and Lissie, my new friends – I hadn't thought about London for quite a while.

'OK,' said Philip, when the queue had dwindled to just a few latecomers and the odd car. 'Go and have fun. Got some money? ' He pulled out a handful of cash, mostly pound coins. He grinned at me and I felt a rush of something I hadn't really felt before. I wasn't sure what it was, but it felt good.

Ryan
There were five of them on duty for the first arrivals in the parking field. Josh, Jake, Melanie, Jasmine and himself. The field had been marked off in rows, with one row to be filled before starting on the next, and the cars would be quite tightly packed. Josh and Jake were old hands, and they took the lead, beckoning the cars into place, telling the drivers to re-park if they weren't close enough.

'Don't any of them get annoyed with you?' Ryan asked.

Jake laughed. 'No, although some of the drivers do get a bit nervous when you ask them to move closer. You have to be firm with them.'

Within an hour there was only a handful of spaces left, and Josh, Melanie and Jasmine went off to enjoy spending their money. Jake stayed behind with me.

'My Dad says you'll be going to our school, Redmond House,' he said.

'That's yours? Yes, we're all starting there next term.'

'D'you play football? Are you any good?'

Ryan thought about lying, but he knew he'd be found out at his first game. 'Actually, I'm rubbish!'

Jake laughed. 'Me too! Music's my thing.'

'Mine's art.' He smiled at Jake. He'd made his first friend.

Simon came half an hour later. 'Philip doesn't think anyone else will be coming. You can come back now.'

'Got any money?' asked Philip when Ryan found him.

'A bit.'

'Have some more!' Philip passed over a handful of silver. 'This is a spend, spend, spend day. What about you, Jake?'

'My Dad's given me plenty. Where are the others?'

'Lissie's entered Biscuit for the Dog Show, Melanie and Jasmine are on the carousel, I think, and I've no idea where Josh is. Caroline's got her own cookie stall over in the far corner – and your parents are around somewhere, Jake. Go and have fun!'

It *was* fun to have money to spend, to buy unlimited

amounts of food – hotdogs, popcorn, a toffee apple, candyfloss – until he was almost sick, to win a teddy bear on a coconut shy (which he planned to give to Biscuit to cuddle with at night), but all the time he was searching the crowds for Joe. Was he there? Was he already talking to Caroline or Philip, telling lies to extract money from them, perhaps even planning to embarrass them by making a scene in front of everybody. If he found Joe, what would he do? What *could* he do?

But by three o'clock he began to relax. The Fete would end at four o'clock, everyone would go home and if Joe turned up after that, Philip – or even Ryan himself – could call the police.

In his search he had been wandering in the direction of the car park again. There were already gaps there. Not everyone had planned to stay until the end. In the far corner of the field, in the last row, he saw a latecomer, an open top sports car, flashing scarlet in the afternoon sun. He had never been particularly drawn to cars, most of Maggie Mum's and Joe's neighbours having nothing beyond cheap old family models. But this one was a beauty.

He had reached it and was caressing the cream leather of the seats when someone spoke behind him.

'Like it? 1967 Jaguar E-Type. Nought to sixty in ten seconds.'

'That's over fifty years old – and it still goes?'

'Of course it goes. Like the wind. It's a very special car.'

The owner leaned forward to stroke the body work. He was tall, wearing a cream linen suit and a matching cream panama hat. Dark sunglasses and the brim of the hat hid his face.

'So, which twin are you?' he asked.

Ryan sighed. Since the television interview everyone seemed to know who he was. Who Simon was. Fame? He could do without it. 'I'm Ryan,' he said.

'You messaged me.' The man took off his sunglasses.

Ryan felt the shock run through him. This was him. Here! His father, here, talking to him!

'You didn't answer!'

The man, his father, shrugged. 'I never answer FB messages. You could have been anyone – someone wanting to get money out of me. Still, I'm here now. You can tell me what you *do* want.'

'Just – Just to know you. You're my father – and you're an artist. I'm an artist too.'

'O.K. Let's get to know each other. Let's get out of here and have a chat. Fancy a ride?'

'I'd better tell Caroline first.'

'She knows,' said Oliver. 'We had a chat earlier.'

'What about Simon? You're his father too.'

Oliver waved a hand at the car. 'It's only a two seater. Another time, eh?'

Ryan hesitated. Surely Caroline would have come along for this first meeting? But perhaps she was too busy running her Cakes and Cookies stall.

His father looked at his watch. 'It's OK, I'll have you back in half an hour.'

This was his father, and his chance to find out more about him. And the car – it was fantastic.

'OK,' he said.

TWENTY FOUR

Simon

It had been a great day, but now the stalls were being dismantled, everything unsold repacked into boxes and vans, the carousel, star of the day, taken apart (watched closely by Lissie), and then there was just the boring job of picking up litter and emptying bins. Josh and Jake and their parents had gone, but Mum had invited Melanie and Jasmine, with their parents, to stay for dinner.

'Anyone seen Ryan?' asked Philip. 'He's not still in the car park, is he?'

But none of us had seen him in the past hour. I phoned his number. There was no reply.

'I'll go and check,' I said. But the car park was empty.

'Perhaps he's in his room,' said Lissie. But he was not there either.

'Has anyone upset him?' asked Mum.

'He wouldn't take off. Not now. Not without telling anyone.'

'I'll check if his bike's still in the garage,' said Lissie, but she was back in minutes. 'It's still there.'

'So where is he?'

We phoned his number. Over and over, but there

was no reply. We checked every field. We checked the barn and all the sheds, and the old cottage. No sign of him. Mum was looking very pale, and Philip put his arm round her. 'He'll be around somewhere. Don't worry. He wouldn't run away again.'

'We should call all the stall holders,' said Mum. 'And our friends. Someone must have seen him.'

'Is there anything we can do?' asked Melanie's mother.

'No, I don't think so – Oh, but I was going to cook you dinner -'

'No, no. We'll go, you mustn't worry about us, but if we see him – on the way home – or if for some reason he's gone back there -'

Melanie touched Philip's arm. Her face was pale. 'Joe's back. D'you think -'

'Let's go home,' said her father. 'I don't know where Joe's staying, but I'll check all his old pub mates – and we'll keep in touch -'

'Yes, thank you,' said Philip.

'I think we should phone the police, although they're probably sick of us by now,' said Mum, after they'd gone.

'We'll have a last look around the farm,' said Philip. 'Simon, Lissie, you can help.'

But Ryan was nowhere. And when we got back, Mum was sitting at the kitchen table, the phone still in her hand. She had been crying.

'The police are putting out an alert, but they were quite impatient with me.'

The phone rang. I picked it up.

'It's Josh here. Our Dad told us you're looking for Ryan. I don't know if it's any help, but I saw him in the car park after most of the cars had gone. He was talking to someone – a man. I only noticed because of the car, a bright red open top sports car.'

'What was the man like?'

'Tall, very smart. He had sunglasses and a hat, so I couldn't really see his face.'

'Thanks, Josh. I'll tell Mum and Philip. They'll probably call you back.'

I put the phone down. I had a horrible feeling I knew who the man was.

'Mum. Philip. There's something I should tell you.'

Lissie wouldn't let me take all the blame.

'Ryan was so insistent,' she said. 'But we never thought he'd try to contact him – and I'm sure Ryan wouldn't have asked him to come here – or even have given our address.'

'He wouldn't have needed to,' said Philip. 'After that television interview, everyone knows who we are and how to find us – and today, the Fete, with hundreds of people milling around – what better place to – to - '

'Kidnap my son,' whispered Mum. 'But why would Oliver want him? After all these years, a son he's never seen and whose mother he abandoned? And where has he taken him?' she asked.

None of us had an answer.

She scrubbed at her tears. 'I'm going to make a pot of tea.'

'He may have gone willingly,' said Philip, while she was gone.

'But just for a ride in a special car,' I said. 'Not for good. I'm so sorry. We should have told you.'

'Perhaps we can trace him through the car, if it was

something unusual.' Philip put his phone on loudspeaker and called Josh. 'Any idea what sort of car it was?' he asked him.

'I've been checking on Google,' said Josh. 'I'm not sure but Dad and I think it might have been a Jaguar, – an E-Type, my Dad said, an old model. They don't make them any more, not since 1968.'

'Thank you, Josh, that's really helpful. There can't be that many registered in the UK. Hopefully this will help us.'

So it was yet another wait, while the local police checked the registers, but with Oliver Daizley's name and the make of car, they eventually came up with an address in London. Another wait while the London police called at the house. His cleaner answered the door. She told them Mr Daizley was away at one of his exhibitions. In Birmingham. She had no idea when he'd be back. She just had orders to clean the place once a week.

'We saw the gallery – and the photograph of him,' said Lissie. 'We can find it again.'

By now the gallery was closed, but there was a number for the owner, who was not pleased to be disturbed late in the evening and had no idea where Oliver was staying. But at least he had Oliver's mobile phone number. Philip phoned the number a dozen times in the next half hour but no one answered. Meanwhile, Lissie and I had found a list of Birmingham hotels ('Bound to be an expensive one', Lissie thought) and called to see if Oliver was staying there. But he wasn't known at any of them.

'Time to bring in the police again,' he said. 'The Birmingham lot.'

'But by now he and Ryan could be anywhere,' said Mum.

Outside the house was silence and darkness, but none of us wanted to go to bed.

Ryan

It was a thrilling ride. Ryan couldn't quite read the speedometer but they must be going at close to a hundred miles an hour, he thought. Oliver was weaving in and out of the other cars, and at any moment Ryan expected to hear the wail of a police siren, but Oliver wasn't slowing down.

He looked at his watch. They had been driving for more than half an hour and he had no idea where they were. Definitely on a motorway, but which one? He tried to read some of the signs but they were there and gone before he could make any sense of them.

'I think we should turn back now,' he shouted to Oliver. 'They'll be wondering where I am.'

'You're a little worrier, aren't you?' Oliver shouted back. 'I'm just going to show you where I'm living, and then – well, we'll see, won't we?'

Ryan wished he would slow down. The thrill of the car and its speed were long gone, he had no idea where he was, and he wanted to go home. Home. The farm. Philip. Caroline. They would be worrying about him

They were on the M6 motorway, he realised after a while. Oliver had been forced to slow down by the volume of traffic, and Ryan could read the signs but none of them meant anything to him. Then a larger sign appeared, and at the top he read 'Birmingham'.

Birmingham. That was where Oliver's exhibition

was being held. But he didn't want to go to an exhibition. He wanted to go home. He took out his phone and started to dial Philip's number.

'I'll have that,' said Oliver, and took the phone from him. 'Too distracting in busy traffic.'

'I'd like to go home,' Ryan said. 'Please.'

But Oliver didn't answer.

Shortly before Birmingham they left the motorway and the roads became narrower. Ryan tried to memorise some of the place names but he was tired, and also feeling rather sick. He tried to remember what he had eaten since breakfast. Two hotdogs, candyfloss, a bag of fudge, popcorn – he couldn't remember any more but they were all going to come up again if Oliver carried on driving.

'I think I'm going to be sick,' he shouted above the noise of the engine.

Oliver didn't comment, just reached behind him and pulled out a plastic carrier bag.

'Use that.'

Ryan felt cold and sweaty after he'd been sick. He wanted to cry. He wanted to be back home with Caroline and Philip and Simon and Lissie. Not here. He wished he had never contacted Oliver. Why had he been so stupid? Why had he thought Oliver might want to meet him? But Oliver *had* met him.

Why? Why?

He closed his eyes and tried to think about nice things. Seeing Lissie's face when she unwrapped his manga comic. Seeing the new school and knowing he would be going there with Simon and Lissie. Talking to Jake and finding out they both hated football. Cleaning out the chicken shed with Philip. Meeting

Aunt Deborah and exploring her motor van.

He dozed off, and only awoke when the car slowed to a more normal speed.

Simon

The room was in darkness when I woke up. Outside, the moon was half hidden behind clouds and nothing was stirring. Lissie was asleep on the floor, her head resting on one of my feet. At first I thought Mum and Philip were awake. They were sitting on the sofa together, holding hands, but their eyes were closed and I could hear a faint snoring from Philip.

I checked my watch. Two a.m. There had been no messages from any of the police. Or from Ryan. I crept out to the kitchen and rang his number. It seemed his phone was out of order.

Where was he? What was happening to him?

Lissie had woken and followed me into the kitchen. She closed the door gently, then poured milk into a pan.

'I'm making cocoa. Want some?'

'No. Yes. OK.'

'D'you think your father really has got Ryan?'

'I can't think of another explanation.'

'We should never have looked him up. Ryan might not have found him on his own.'

'No.'

She stared into the pan of milk until it began to boil up, and then she turned it off.

'You don't think his father will hurt him, do you?'

'We don't know anything about him really, do we?'

The door opened and Mum came in. 'I was thinking. That nice man at the BBC. I could ask him to put a message on TV, asking if anyone's seen the car, and if so, where?'

'Good idea, Mum. We could try that.'

'Would you like some cocoa?' asked Lissie.

'Yes, please.' Mum looked around vaguely. 'And I think there are some cookies. Somewhere.'

We ate cookies to please her, and then Philip appeared, looking haggard and bleary-eyed.

'No messages?'

'No,' I said.

'You should all go to bed,' said Mum. 'You'll need your strength for tomorrow.'

'You should, too,' said Lissie.

'I can't. I have to be here. Awake. In case – in case we hear something.' She began to sob, and Philip put his arms around her.

Waiting. Not knowing. It was horrible. And there was nothing we could do.

Ryan

The roads were very narrow now, bordered by hedges and gardens and small houses, with just an occasional street light. One of the lights was outside a shop. Ryan squinted to read the lettering above it. 'Whitchurch Post Office'. He repeated the name to himself silently, over and over.

About a mile further on Oliver turned on to a broad drive. It led to a large unlit house, partially hidden by tall mature trees.

'Out you get,' he said.

'Is this your house?' asked Ryan.

'Just while the exhibition was on. Belongs to a friend of mine. Come on in, I'll show you round.'

The front door opened into a large hall. Oliver switched on a light, and Ryan saw the walls were hung with a dozen or more paintings, mostly landscapes.

'Are these his paintings?'

Oliver nodded. 'D'you like them?'

'They're lovely,' said Ryan, but Oliver dismissed them. 'Chocolate box stuff. He'll never be a real artist.' Her indicated a group of paintings stacked up in a corner. 'Those are mine.'

'Didn't you sell any?'

'Of course I did. Over 70 per cent.'

It's getting late. Shouldn't we get back?'

'Aren't you interested?'

'Of course – but I'd better phone Caroline and Philip. They'll be getting worried.'

'Oh, I left your phone in the car – I'll go and fetch it.'

As Oliver walked over to the car, Ryan wondered if he could sneak off, find his way to the village they'd passed, and knock on someone's door. But Oliver was already on his way back.

Just before he reached the house he dropped the phone and appeared to stumble.

'Oh dear me, I've trodden on it!' He picked up the pieces and stared at them. 'Sorry, Ryan, looks as if it's broken. Never mind, *I'll* phone Caroline. It's pretty late now, I'll tell her we'll be back tomorrow.'

Ryan didn't believe him. He didn't believe anything Ryan said now. And he was scared. Really scared.

TWENTY FIVE

Ryan

'You can sleep in here. Next to the bathroom, in case you're sick again', said Oliver. He opened one of the doors to reveal a small room with a single bed, a small cabinet alongside, a chair and a wardrobe. The bed was made up with pillows and a duvet but it was clearly a room that was not used very often. There was nothing personal, apart from one of the owner's landscapes above the headboard. There was no phone.

'I suppose you're hungry. I didn't stock much. I eat out most of the time, but we can do beans on toast, I suppose. Will that do?'

The thought of food, any food, made bile rise in Ryan's throat again, but he nodded. Perhaps Oliver would leave him alone, and then he could open a window, climb out, down a rainpipe or something, call for help – although he hadn't noticed any other houses nearby.

'My friend – Lucas – is away a lot, which is how I come to be using his house. He has a very sophisticated alarm system installed. Can't even touch a window, inside or out, without knowing the code,' said Oliver, as if reading Ryan's mind.

After he'd gone, Ryan went to the bathroom. There

was a window in there, too, but quite small. The top was already open, but the space wouldn't allow anything larger than a kitten to climb through. There was a bolt on the inside of the door and he slid it across, but what good would that do? It would be stalemate, wouldn't it? Oliver outside, Ryan inside and still trapped. And Oliver didn't own the house, so he probably wouldn't kick the door down as they did in films.

'What do you want?' he whispered later, when he sat opposite Oliver in the kitchen and pretended to eat, moving the beans around on his piece of toast.

'Want? Just to get to know you. See if we suit.'

'Suit?'

Oliver put down his knife and fork.

'I was married. Stunning woman but always there, wanting this, wanting that, nagging. Wanting babies. I never wanted babies, they mess up your life. But you – ready made, a sensible age. I watched the interview Caroline did. There you were, you and the other kid, both looking like me, both with my artistic genes. I thought, *Maybe that would work.* You could be my assistant, I could teach you all I know. I'm good, I've got a reputation and I make pots of money.'

'So why did you choose me, and not Simon?'

Oliver shrugged. 'Either of you would have done, but Simon – Caroline's had him from the start, there'd have been more fuss, wouldn't there? And I'd have had trouble persuading him to leave. But you – a loner, a persistent runaway, no real ties to Caroline or her family – contacting me out of the blue - you were easier. And there you were, in the car park, nobody about. It was what they call serendipity.'

'I don't know what that means.'

'It means finding good things by accident. And although I'd made a few plans, I didn't expect it to be quite as easy as you made it!'

'But – I never meant – I just wanted to get to know you. I never meant to leave Caroline and Philip and Simon and Lissie! I – I love them!'

And it was true. He just hadn't fully realised it until this moment, when all that was in danger. He *did* love them. And it no longer felt as if he was being disloyal to Maggie Mum. There was room for them all in his heart.

'How can you love them? You've only known them a few weeks.'

'Let me go. Please!'

'Bit late now, my boy. You'd cry kidnap and I'd be arrested.'

'You wouldn't be, I promise. I'd tell them I wanted to go with you, but I changed my mind. Please! Take me back!'

But Oliver wasn't looking at me. He continued to eat, scraping the last few beans and crumbs of toast into his mouth.

'Too late, Ryan. Too late.'

Simon

Mum looked ill the next morning. She wandered backwards and forwards across the kitchen, picking up the kettle and putting it down again, staring at a loaf of bread, then putting it back in the bread bin.

'Sit down,' said Philip. 'I'll make you some strong coffee. Anyone else? You should all eat. And drink.

We need to be ready for action, if the police find anything.'

'Is it my fault?' Mum asked. 'I shouldn't have arranged that television interview. Oliver wouldn't have known anything about him if it wasn't for me.'

'It's not your fault, Mum. Ryan *wanted* to contact him.'

'I'll phone the police again – Liverpool *and* Birmingham. See if they've learned anything overnight,' said Philip.

But the gallery owner phoned first. 'I remembered something,' he said. 'I think Oliver mentioned staying at a friend's house while the owner was on holiday. Near one of the villages, he said, but I can't remember if he said which one.'

'Thank you,' said Philip. 'I'll pass that on to the police.'

'So what can *we* do?' I asked.

'I don't know. I don't know.'

'I'm going to look up all the villages around Birmingham and make a list,' said Lissie.

Then Mum's phone rang. She stared at it, afraid to answer. I grabbed it.

'Hello! Police?'

'What? No, it's me, Aunt Deborah. Is that you, Ryan? Or Simon?'

'It's me, Simon. Ryan's not here. He's – he's -' I looked over at Mum. She nodded.

'He's been kidnapped! We think Oliver Daizley, his father, has got him?'

There was silence for several seconds. Then, 'So why aren't you all out searching for him?'

'We don't know where to start. The police -'

'Useless lot. Right, I'm on my way! Tell your Mum!'

'Give me the phone!' said Mum, but too late.

'Aunt Deborah's on her way,' I told her.

I think we all felt comforted, even though there was nothing she could do that the police weren't already doing.

Later Melanie's father phoned. He had traced Joe. 'I spoke to Gary, his mate. Seems Joe had been living with his sister, but she chucked him out because of his heavy drinking. So he came back here and landed on Gary's doorstep. I think Gary's planning to chuck him out, too, but he was reasonably sure Joe hadn't taken Ryan. The last thing he wanted was to have the police after him.'

'Thank you,' said Philip, 'but we think now that Ryan's real father has taken him. We don't know why, and we don't know if Ryan went willingly.'

'Will Ryan's father go to prison if he's found?' I asked, when Philip had finished the call.

'I don't know,' he said. 'I don't understand any of this. Why would he want him after all these years?'

I opened my laptop and googled Oliver's name again. There were quite a few entries for him, and we hadn't looked far beyond the Birmingham gallery entry, but there was nothing helpful.

I went back to his Facebook page. No personal information, no friends, nothing. I started browsing through the photographs of his paintings. Not all were portraits. There were several landscapes and townscapes – and against most of the paintings Oliver had posted a caption. The name of the sitter, the whereabouts of the landscapes, the name of the town.

Several of the paintings were of somewhere called Carmel. I looked it up. It was near San Francisco, and seemed to be a favourite place for artists, with lots of galleries.

There were three paintings of a house. It looked like many of the others in Carmel. And there was a caption: My new base.

'Philip. Mum. Come and see this. Do you think he's hoping to take Ryan to America?'

They stared at the photographs.

'It wouldn't be that easy,' said Philip. 'He would have to get a passport for him – that's even if Ryan agreed.'

'But he wouldn't, would he?' Mum whispered. 'He wouldn't want to leave us.'

I couldn't look at her. I was so full of rage. How could Ryan do this to her? How could he hurt her – us – after we'd all done so much for him?

Ryan

Sometime in the early hours of the morning he had fallen asleep. He dreamed a crazy dream. He was riding on Sidney's back and Oliver, in his E-type Jaguar, was chasing him across the fields. Ryan was winning, because Sidney happily crashed through hedges but Oliver didn't want to get his car scratched and was falling behind, until all Ryan could hear was his voice, faintly calling him.

'Ryan! Wake up. Breakfast!'

His eyes were heavy, and the thought of food brought back an urge to be sick. Oliver knocked on the bedroom door.

'I'm coming!'

Breakfast was toast again, and orange juice.

'I'll order pizzas for lunch,' said Oliver. 'Get them delivered.'

'I'm not hungry.'

Oliver stared at him silently, and then he got up and fetched something from his coat pocket. His phone. Ryan stared at it. If only he could get his hands on it.

'May I have a photo of you?' Oliver asked. Without waiting for permission he took one. 'Hmm, not bad. Want a look?' He turned the phone briefly towards Ryan, then began pressing buttons.

'Got something to show you.' Oliver passed the phone to him. 'Carmel, California. That's my future. And that's my new house there. You'd like it. Art galleries on every block, every tenth person is an artist or wants to buy art. And I can teach you.'

'But why? I don't understand. You said you don't like babies. Why do you want me?' Ryan was still holding the phone. Slowly he lowered his hand until it was level with the table edge, then below the edge. 'I'd only be a nuisance, wouldn't I?'

Oliver looked away. 'It could be good. I've been on my own a long time. Five years. But I don't want to get married again – and I wouldn't be any good with young children. But when I saw you – and Simon – on television, I thought – that could work. Caroline can keep Simon, and I could have you. A new life – for you, and for me too. In a new fabulous place where we could have fun and make lots of money. You'd love it.'

Under the table Ryan fingered the buttons on the phone. If only he could phone someone. But the only number he could remember was Maggie Mum's, and that wouldn't reach anyone. Nine nine nine. Yes, he'd phone the police – but what could he tell them? Then he remembered the name on the village post office they had passed. Whitchurch. Yes! But it was too late. Oliver was staring at him. Frowning.

'I'll have my phone back,' he said. 'Now!'

Simon

We didn't know what to do next. We had told the police they needed to check all the villages around Birmingham.

'That's a tall order,' they said. 'Don't you have any idea *which* village?'

'If we knew that,' said Philip coldly, 'we'd be driving up there and searching ourselves!'

Lissie went out to the kitchen and collected Biscuit from his dog bed. She curled up on the sofa and cuddled the puppy close to her. Then she said, 'I don't think Ryan chose to go with his father. I think maybe his father just offered him a ride in his big posh car and – Well, what would *you* have done, Simon? You wouldn't have turned down a ride, would you?'

'If I knew the driver was my real father, who'd never wanted to know me, yes, I would!'

'I think Ryan just expected it to be a short ride – up the motorway to the next junction, then back. Home in time for tea,' said Lissie.

We were all quiet after that, thinking about Oliver. None of us knew what he was like. Not even Mum. The Oliver she had known when she was seventeen was not the same Oliver as now, thirteen years later. I wondered how Ryan was feeling. Was he scared? Did I care?

Ryan

Oliver had been on the phone in his bedroom for nearly an hour, making one call after another. Ryan suspected they had to do with him taking Ryan to America, to the town with all the artists, where Oliver seemed to think they'd be happy ever after. He guessed Oliver had plenty of money. He could probably arrange a passport quite easily. After all, he was his father, his *real* father, so who would ask questions?

But Ryan didn't want to go to America. He didn't want to fly thousands of miles across the Atlantic with a father that he hardly knew, that he was a little scared of. He wanted to go home.

Home. The farm. It *was* his home now, and that's where he wanted to be.

He crept out into the hall and listened. Oliver was still talking, his voice raised, impatient. He tiptoed over to the front door. He touched it, a featherlight touch. What would it take, how much pressure, to set off the alarm?

He stared around the hall. A house like this, on its own, at least a mile, he guessed, from the nearest village – surely it would have a landline. But there was no sign of one. There were hangers for coats on one wall, and alongside them a table. Nothing on it except a notepad and a pen. He crouched down and looked underneath the table. And there it was. A connection for a telephone. But where was the phone? Had Oliver hidden it?

There was no other furniture in the hall, but there was a cupboard beneath the stairs. Quietly, holding his breath, he opened its door. And there was the telephone. It was hidden beneath a roughly folded travelling rug, but a telltale loop of cable was still uncovered.

Praying that Oliver still had calls to make, Ryan plugged the phone into its connection, and listened. Yes, he was getting a signal. He could ring home. But what was the number? He couldn't remember. *He couldn't remember!*

He would have to phone the police.

'My name is Ryan -' Should he say McKenna? Or had Caroline already changed it to Keyes? He gave them both. 'and I'm at a big house near a village called Whitchurch. I've been taken from my home. I think my family will be looking for me. I'm with a man called Oliver Daizley. Please come and get me!'

He could hardly breathe. Had Oliver heard him? Quickly, he unplugged the telephone, replaced it in the understair cupboard, and crept up to his bedroom.

He was sweating. Any moment Oliver might come out of his room. He pulled a grubby tissue from the pocket of his jeans and scrubbed at his face.

Five minutes later he heard Oliver on the stairs. His door opened.

'All done!,' said Oliver. 'Passport, plane tickets, the lot! We leave in the morning.'

'How could you get a passport so quickly?'

Oliver touched his nose. 'Connections. And money. It's coming by courier.'

'What about clothes?' Ryan asked. 'I don't even have a jacket.'

Oliver waved a hand impatiently. 'We'll pick up all we need at the airport.' He took a big breath and smiled, his eyes alight. 'Right! Pizzas should be here any time now. Hungry?'

TWENTY SIX

Ryan

Ryan took a sip of the orange juice Oliver had poured. He stared at the pizza in front of him, ham and pineapple, one of his favourites. He couldn't eat it.

'If you don't want that, I'll have it,' said Oliver. 'But there's not much else in the fridge and I'm not taking any trips to the supermarket.'

Ryan pushed the plate towards him. There was a huge lump of fear in his throat. Would the police take any notice of his call or think it was just a hoax? Even if they'd believed him, how long would it take them to find a big house near Whitchurch? There were probably dozens of them, and they would have to speak with all the owners. It could take hours. Days even. And tomorrow morning he and Oliver would be on a plane to America and it would be too late.

But he could make a fuss at the airport. He could lock himself in a toilet, or run up to one of the officials - did they have airport police? He didn't know. He and Mum never had that kind of holiday, where you took a plane to somewhere hot and sunny, and after they moved to Liverpool they never had holidays at all.

But even if the police came to this house, Oliver might

convince them that his son was just one of those difficult kids and was having a tantrum.

And then, what would he do after the police had gone away? Ryan had no idea, but he was scared.

Oliver had finished the second pizza and was leaning back in his chair, tapping his teeth with the end of his fork.

'What d'you want to do?' he asked. 'Fancy another drive?'

No! Ryan screamed silently. *We have to stay here for the police!*

'I still feel really sick.'

Oliver sighed. 'OK, so what would you like to do?'

Ryan couldn't think of anything. Oliver had risen and was prowling round the kitchen.

'Here's what we'll do,' he said at last. 'We'll go up to Jeremy's studio and we'll paint a portrait of each other – simultaneously. Could be fun?'

'I – I don't really paint. Not oils, anyway. I draw, and I can use coloured inks or watercolours -'

'Ok, that'll do, but when we get to Carmel I'm going to teach you how to use oils.' Oliver stared at him. He was grinning. 'Might even open a gallery to display our works. "Oliver and Ryan Daisley" - "Oliver Daisley and Son". How about that?'

Inside the studio, which had a bare wooden floor, huge uncurtained windows and four easels, Oliver opened a cupboard and pulled out a large board and a large sheet of coloured card. He set them up on one of the easels, then opened a drawer containing a rainbow of colours.

'Ever used pastels?' he asked.

'No, and I've never drawn anything that big before.'

'So, two new experiences for you.' He placed the drawer of pastels on a high stool beside the easel and spent some time demonstrating how to use them. Then he set up another easel at the other end of the room, so that he and Ryan faced each other.

'Ready to start?'

Ryan nodded. He stared at the pastels, a hundred or more sticks, each colour ranging from the palest to the darkest. Despite his fears, his fingers itched to use them.

Simon

Each time the phone rang we all jumped, but it was always Aunt Deborah. 'Any news?' she would ask, and then, 'I'm at Junction 11' – or 'Junction 15' – or 'I'm coming on to the M40 now.'

'She's going to get arrested,' said Philip. 'She must be driving that motor home like a maniac - and phoning at the same time!'

'If only we *had* some news,' said Mum. She sounded calm, but her fingernails had been scratching at the skin on the back of her hands, making them bleed.

At midday she rose and began to prepare lunch. Just bread and cheese, and fruit. Lissie went to help her. None of us ate it.

Melanie phoned me. 'Any news?

Josh and Jake's Dad phoned. 'Any news?'

And Aunt Deborah again. 'Any news?'

Through the open window we could hear the cows mooing.

'Damn, I forgot the milking,' said Philip

'We'll help,' said Lissie. She glared at me. 'Won't we?

'Of course,' I said. I was glad to have something to do. We had been in that room for hours, just waiting and worrying.

'You all right, Mum?' I asked. 'I'll stay if you want me.'

'No. You go,' she whispered.

There was something about the milking parlour that was calming, peaceful. We didn't speak to each other. It was just good to be away from the house and to be able to concentrate on something else – although we'd all brought our phones with us.

Philip and Lissie knew the names of all the cows and spoke to them as they entered the stalls. I stared at the cow who was heading towards my end of the parlour. Her soft brown lash-framed eyes stared back at me.

'That's Maisie,' said Lissie.

'How do you know?' I asked her. 'They're all brown and white.'

'If you were with a group of friends who all had blonde hair and blue eyes, would you be able to tell the difference?'

'Of course.'

'Well, then!'

I was sorry when the milking ended. It would be back to the house, and the waiting.

Ryan
He loved using the pastels, they were so soft and so

creamy, and the colours so rich. He wondered if they were very expensive. He would love to own his own set. Perhaps Philip and Caroline would buy them for him. If he was ever to see them again, that is. He had been holding the stick of pastel too tightly and it broke and fell to the floor.

'How's it going?' asked Oliver. 'Want any help?'

'No, it's fine.' And actually, despite using a medium that he had never tried before, his portrait of Oliver was quite a good likeness. It was strange. In studying his father's face, analysing his features, getting his expression in the shape of his eyes, the curve of his mouth, he had begun to lose his fear of him. There was something in his father's face that he had seen in his own face at times when he had looked into a mirror.

He stepped back from the easel. 'I think I'm finished.'

Oliver came over and stood beside him, a hand laid lightly on Ryan's shoulder.

'That is good. Very good,' he said, after a long silence. 'You're a true artist, Ryan. Want to see yours?'

Oliver had painted a full length portrait of Ryan. Leaning in towards his easel, his lips pursed, his eyes narrowed, full of concentration.

'Is that how I look?' he asked.

The hand squeezed his shoulder. 'Yes.'

They stared at each other, father and son, for a long

moment.

'I'm glad we've met,' Oliver said. 'And I'm sorry about the past. I hope I can make up for it now.'

And then the doorbell rang.

Simon

It was late in the afternoon when the call came to Philip's phone. We couldn't hear what was said but we knew it was important. Philip had jerked upright, and was now pacing the room, firing questions into the phone. And then he turned to us.

'That was the police. They've found him! They've got Oliver too. They're at the Birmingham HQ. Oliver's under arrest and Ryan's being interviewed. He's safe, and he's OK.'

Mum looked as if she was going to faint.

'When can we have him back?' she asked.

'I don't know – they didn't say -'

'I'm going to phone Aunt Deborah. She must be near Birmingham now. I'll ask her to go straight to the station. Perhaps she can bring him home!'

'They may not let her take him. He may have to stay until charges have been made -'

'They can't keep him overnight, he's only a child. Anyway, no one wins against Aunt Deborah.'

'OK, phone her – but tell her to slow down once she's got Ryan in the van!'

Mum turned to us, beaming. 'He could be home in a couple of hours!'

Ryan

They didn't want him to see Oliver again. They had asked him dozens of questions, maybe a hundred or more. Some he didn't want to answer, because now he was safe the past twenty four hours or so didn't seem as frightening as they had at the time. And Oliver hadn't harmed him, he had just wanted to be his father. *Better late than never,* Ryan thought to himself. But no, it *was* too late.

On the other hand, he didn't want Oliver to go to prison.

He heard Aunt Deborah before he saw her. She was arguing with the desk sergeant, who Ryan remembered was quite a small man. Aunt Deborah would be towering over him, speaking slowly in that clear, loud, teacher's voice that no one dared contradict.

And then she was in the back office where he had been sitting with a female officer, and he was enveloped. She was warm and safe and she smelled of peppermints and black coffee and doughnuts, whatever she had been nibbling on to keep her going on the drive to the police station.

'I'm taking you home, young man!' she said.

But when she released him, he turned to the police officer. 'Can I see Oliver before I go?' he asked.

'Surely not?' said Aunt Deborah, but he turned to the officer again.

'Please?'

They allowed him two minutes in Oliver's cell. Oliver said nothing, and Ryan just stood there until he was called. But as he turned away, Oliver called, 'I'm sorry. Truly.'

'I hope you don't get into too much trouble,' Ryan said as he left.

He didn't think he could sleep on the way back to the farm, but he did, and only woke when the motor home pulled to a stop and Aunt Deborah gently shook his shoulder.

'You're home, Ryan!'

Simon

Mum had prepared a celebration dinner, but once again it was wasted. We were all too stressed to eat. Lissie and Mum were sobbing, Ryan was sobbing, Philip kept clearing his throat and blinking hard. Aunt Deborah wasn't sobbing. She was sitting erect at the table, smiling triumphantly as if she personally had engineered Ryan's rescue.

Me? I was determined not to cry. I even managed to cut a piece of steak and carry it to my mouth, but I couldn't swallow it. I didn't know what to feel. There was relief, but the rage was still there too.

I had been so worried while Ryan was gone, wanting him safe and home for Mum's sake, but now he was back, all my mixed and muddled feelings were back too. Even before he had contacted Oliver, there were problems. Whenever he was around, I somehow felt displaced, at the back of the queue. I knew everything had been worse for Ryan. He'd lost his Maggie-Mum, he'd lost his home – but I'd lost things too, when Mum had met Philip and brought me here, leaving behind my city life, my friends, my school.

I felt ashamed to compare our lives, but there it was – I couldn't help myself.

Mum whispered something to Lissie before going back to the kitchen. Lissie went over to the door and switched off all the lights. Then Mum was back, bearing a huge Baked Alaska, one of her specialties. It was studded with a dozen or more candles, their glow lighting the table.

'Here's to the return of our almost lost one.' She carried the cake round to Ryan's seat and placed it before him. 'We love you, Ryan.'

Hear, hear! They all cheered, and I joined in. But I couldn't eat the cake.

TWENTY SEVEN

Ryan

The talk had moved on to Oliver. They were saying horrible things about him and expecting Ryan to join in, but he couldn't.

'Anyway, you're safe now,' said Caroline. 'Nothing can hurt you. Oliver can't hurt you.'

'I don't think he would have done. He just – he wanted to open a gallery in America. Him and me. "Oliver Daizley and Son", he was going to call it.'

They were all staring at him now.

'You didn't *like* him, did you?' asked Simon.

'No! Of course not!' But he hadn't hated him either. And that afternoon, when the police came – Oliver's face, his expression . . .

Caroline looked at her watch. 'Bedtime!' she said.

'It's only nine thirty,' Simon protested.

'But it's been a long, long day, and none of us slept last night. Aunt Deborah – you must be exhausted after that long drive. And Ryan – what about you?'

'I *am* tired.' He stood up. "I didn't sleep much. I – I

didn't know what was going to happen. Am I still in the same room?' he asked Caroline.

'Or you can have the other bed in the van,' said Aunt Deborah quickly.

'Yes, please.'

'Lucky thing!' said Lissie.

'Your turn will come,' said Aunt Deborah. 'I'm planning to stay a few days – until this thing is sorted.'

'What about your job?' asked Philip.

'We haven't got a production this week, and I've delegated some of the tasks for the following week. Besides, I want to be here when the police come. The Birmingham lot didn't really want to let Ryan go, but they've agreed to have him interviewed again by the Liverpool police.'

'Poor Ryan,' said Lissie.

'Well, we'll all be here to support him.'

Ryan still hadn't said anything.

'So, young man, go and get your things,' said Aunt Deborah, 'and we'll see the rest of you in the morning.'

Simon

After Aunt Deborah had taken Ryan off to the van Mum asked us to stay a few minutes.

'Do you think Ryan is OK? He was so quiet.'

'He usually is,' said Lissie.

'I think he's still shocked. It must have been a

terrifying experience.'

'But he didn't tell us *anything*,' I said.

'And Aunt Deborah said he insisted on seeing Oliver before they left the police station. I wonder why?'

'Well, we'll find out more tomorrow. Let's hope they don't send Sergeant Bill to interview him,' said Philip.

'I still don't think it was him who told the Press,' said Mum. 'They all have to fill in reports, don't they? Any one of them could have done it.'

'Can we all be there when they're interviewing Ryan?' asked Lissie.

'Oh no. There has to be a responsible adult when someone Ryan's age is interviewed, but not other children,' said Philip.

'But we could tell them about finding Ryan and Simon's father online, and Ryan sending him messages -'

'*What?*' Philip was on his feet.

'I – we didn't want to tell you – about the messages,' I said. 'I thought you might be angry.'

'But this explains a lot. He could argue that Ryan invited him. Perhaps Ryan *did* invite him.'

'He didn't. Not exactly. Ryan sent three messages but he didn't get a reply to any of them.'

'He must have heard about the Fete,' said Philip. 'And of course he probably saw your interview on television, Carrie.'

Mum stood up and began to gather our used plates. 'Oh, so *I'm* to blame, am I?'

We were all in danger of quarrelling.

'No one's to blame,' said Philip. 'Except Oliver Daizley. Now, let's all go to bed. We're all tired. We don't want to start fighting.'

Although none of us had slept in the past twenty four hours, I lay awake for a long time, feeling more and more angry. Mum was blaming Oliver Daizley, but it was Ryan who had upset everyone. I wished he was in the room next door, so that I could go and talk with him alone, find out exactly what had happened. Ryan was always the quiet one, but tonight he'd acted as if he was carrying a secret. What was it? Was he silent because nothing had happened, or because it was all too awful and he just wanted to forget?

Ryan

'So,' said Aunt Deborah, when they were in their beds. 'Is there anything you want to say?' She waited. 'You don't have to talk, you know. Not to me, not to the family – but you will have to talk to the police tomorrow.'

'What will happen to him? Will he go to prison?'

'I don't know, Ryan. Possibly. He took you away without permission – from your mother or from you yourself. That's called abduction. And he frightened you.'

'Not at the end. Only at the beginning.'

'But he planned to take you abroad, didn't he? And you're under sixteen. Even if you wanted to go with him, he would still have needed your mother's permission.'

'So he'll be punished.'

'I expect so, but see what the police say tomorrow. And talk to your Mum.'

Aunt Deborah rose. 'Now, time to sleep. I hope you don't snore. I think snores might ricochet around this tiny space and keep me awake!'

He managed a smile as she tucked him in, but he remained awake for another hour. Aunt Deborah had fallen asleep almost instantly. He wondered if he should tell her in the morning about her own snores.

Simon

The doorbell rang at 10 o'clock the next day. Philip went to answer it.

'You!' we heard him say.

'I'm sorry. They sent me because I've been before, and your family knows me.'

It was Sergeant Bill.

Lissie and I had been told to keep out of the way. I waited until Mum and Philip, Aunt Deborah and Ryan had taken him into the sitting room, and firmly shut the door, then beckoned Lissie outside. It was a warm sunny morning and the sitting room windows were partly open. We squatted on the ground just below them.

'How are you?' Bill was asking Ryan.

We could hear quite well, although it was a struggle to hear Ryan's quiet replies. At first Aunt Deborah was answering for him, until Bill shut her up. He asked Ryan to tell him exactly what happened, from the afternoon of the Fete onwards. It was quite a shock to realise that was only two days ago.

'He'd asked me if I wanted a drive in his car, and I said Yes,' Ryan was telling him.

'And did you know then that he was your father?'

'Yes, he'd told me.'

'And when did you start to feel scared?'

'When he wouldn't turn round and bring me back.'

'So, what happened next?'

'I was sick. He gave me a bag to throw up in. But he wouldn't turn round. He said he'd spoken to Caroline and she knew I was with him.'

'That's not true,' Mum said. 'I didn't even know Oliver was at the Fete!'

'So he took you to this house – a friend's house – What happened then?'

'My phone was in the car – he went back for it, but then he tripped and trod on it.'

'You think that was deliberate?'

'Yes.'

'What happened next?'

'We had beans on toast.'

'What next?'

'He said he wanted to get to know me, and he told me a bit about himself. How he'd been married, but not any more, and about not wanting any babies. And how about meeting me was sere – serendipity. And about me living with him in America in some place that was all artists, and how he would open a gallery for our paintings.'

'And then?'

'He showed me the bedroom I'd be sleeping in.'

There was silence for a moment or two. Then Bill started again.

'Was that just a single bedroom?'

'Of course. He wasn't – he just wanted to be my father.'

'And he didn't think he needed to get permission for that?'

'I don't know.'

Mum broke in then: 'Of course he needed permission! Oliver Daizley has never at any time contacted me since I told him I was pregnant.'

'Mr Daizley says he gave you several hundred pounds at the time. Money his father had given him for a skiing holiday.'

'Well, yes, but then within a week or two he'd gone off to University and I never heard from him again.'

'So until recently Mr Daizley didn't actually know there was a baby – two, in fact – and that he was a father?'

'No, I suppose not,' said Mum.

'So, Ryan,' said Bill, 'when you found out his identity, you sent him several messages online.'

'Yes, but he didn't answer.'

'There was no communication until the day of the Fete?'

'No.'

'In taking you away, did he at any time, for any reason, threaten you, Ryan?'

'No.'

'And did he ask if you wanted to got to America?'

'Not exactly – but he thought I'd enjoy it and enjoy being an artist there.'

'What about Simon? Would he have taken him, if he'd been in the car park instead of you?'

Lissie glanced at me, about to speak, but I put my finger

to my lips. I wanted to hear Ryan's answer.

'I don't think so,' Ryan said. 'He said Simon and Caroline were too attached to each other, but I'd only been with them a few weeks, so they wouldn't care.'

'Of course we'd care!' said Mum.

'Ryan's part of our family now,' said Philip.

There was silence for a while, and then Bill spoke again.

'So, Ryan, why do you think Mr Daizley took you away – kidnapped you, in fact? Was it some sort of revenge?'

'No. I think – hearing Caroline say on TV that she'd given me away when I was a baby, and had only just found me again – perhaps he thought that she hadn't wanted me then, and perhaps she only wanted me now because Simon had found me – so he didn't see why he and Caroline shouldn't have one of us each.'

'Why are you defending him, Ryan?' asked Caroline.

'I think he was lonely. I don't think he had anyone of his own. I *was* scared at first, but then – I felt sorry for him – being alone, because, well, I've been alone too. And yesterday afternoon – when we were painting together – we were talking quite a lot, and – I don't know, I felt maybe he would have brought me back. But then the police came.'

There was another long silence after that, and then Bill spoke.

'Well, everything I've heard this morning ties in with Mr Daizley's own story.'

'So, will he go to prison?' asked Philip.

'I can't answer that,' said Bill, 'but I think it might be unlikely.'

We heard all of them rising from their seats after that, and Lissie and I crept away.

Mum and Philip had a long talk after Bill left. We heard them arguing several times, always shutting up when any of us were near, but in the end they told us they were not going to press charges against Oliver.

'There will be conditions, though,' said Mum. 'Oliver is not to contact you again – either of you – until you're eighteen, and then it will be up to you, not him.'

'Does that mean we mustn't write to him either?' asked Ryan.

I glared at him. 'Why would you want to?'

Ryan said nothing.

'You know Philip and I are planning to marry soon,' said Mum, 'and then *he* wants to be your father. All of us, one family.'

Lissie broke the silence. 'I'm going to be bridesmaid!' she said. 'You two can be – what do you call them, Mum?'

'Ushers.'

I glanced at Ryan. For once, I think our expressions matched. I turned away.

TWENTY EIGHT

Ryan

That night Simon came into his room. He didn't knock, just marched in and began pacing around the bed.

'We need to talk.'

'What about?' Ryan put down the magazine he'd been trying to read. This was it. Simon had been boiling over with rage all evening. Ryan was surprised nobody else had commented on it.

'Do you realise how much you upset us all? My Mum especially.'

'She's my Mum too.'

'Yes, your Mum too – except you've never really accepted her. If you had, you wouldn't have been so disloyal. And unkind. Choosing to search for the man who abandoned her! What did you think was going to happen when you sent him those messages?

'I just wanted to know what he was like. What I came from. You'll never understand. When you find out everything about your background is untrue, it's as if – as if you've got no identity, as if you're not a real person. And then there was the television interview, and Caroline saying she'd given me away. I got to thinking, maybe *that* was the truth.'

'She didn't give you away. My Mum lied so that others wouldn't hear and condemn your MaggieMum for stealing you. You should have been grateful. Instead, you throw it in her face and decide to find your father!'

'You were interested too, you can't deny it,' said Ryan.

'But not enough to contact him, to hurt Mum. Sending him all those messages. Inviting him to the Fete, that was really cruel.' Simon leaned over him. He was almost hissing. 'My Mum told lies for you on TV, and look how you've repaid her!'

'I didn't invite him! I just wanted to have some sort of conversation with him. Find out if he'd ever thought about me – us – over the years. I wanted to know what sort of person he was. Maybe to find out what sort of person *I* was.'

'Yeah, well we all know that now, don't we?' Simon sneered. 'Ungrateful. Deceitful. Selfish.'

'I never thought he'd turn up here – and I certainly wouldn't have got in his car if I'd known what he planned.' And then Ryan couldn't stop them. He cursed the tears that had become so easy to shed since MaggieMum and he had left Cornwall.

'Oh, for Pete's sake!' Simon turned away in disgust.

'I'm going to bed!'

Simon

Lissie grabbed me after breakfast the next day.

'Come and help me feed the chickens.'

'Why should I?'

'Because I'm asking you nicely, and I'm saying please, pretty please?'

I sighed. I had no interest in feeding chickens on any morning, but especially not this morning when I was still feeling bad tempered and jangly.

In the yard the chickens heard our footsteps and started clamouring to be freed. Lissie unbolted the door of their shed and stepped aside to avoid the tsunami as they poured out.

'Petronella!' she called. Petronella was her favourite chicken, the one she was holding in my birthday portrait of her, but friendship and loyalty were nothing when there was food to be fought for, and Petronella hardly spared her a glance.

'I heard you last night,' Lissie said.

'I might have known you'd be eavesdropping.'

'I'm surprised Mum and Dad didn't hear you too, the way you were shouting at poor Ryan!'

'Oh, *poor Ryan!* He deserved it.'

'No, he didn't.'

'Oh well, I might have known you'd be on his side, like everyone else.'

'You're just jealous. You brought him here, but now

you think he's getting more attention than you, you don't like it.'

'I'm not jealous. I'm just looking out for Mum!'

'Mum understands. She knows how Joe abused Ryan, and how much worse it got after Ryan's MaggieMum died. Joe beat him up whenever he got drunk, and there was hardly ever anything to eat. Ryan really suffered. There was no one to protect him, and Mum understands how it damaged him and how hard it is now for him to get past it.'

'How do you know all this?'

'Like you said, I'm good at eavesdropping. They were in Ryan's room one day and I listened from the landing.'

'She should have told us. She should have told *me*. I thought -'

'She didn't tell anyone – except maybe my Dad, I suppose. It was Ryan's secret.'

'But I'm his twin. I should have been told.'

'Well, now you know and you can stop being jealous of him, and you can stop shouting at him, can't you? You can try to understand why he can't yet put his trust in any of us, and why he needed to know more about himself – and about Oliver, because he's descended from him too.'

If I'd known, I wouldn't have been so mean to him. I wouldn't have begrudged him getting more attention than me at times. And I wouldn't have scoffed at his tears. I turned and went back to the house, but I couldn't find him. I went back to Lissie.

'Where is he?'

'Gone for a ride. Probably to see Melanie, who's one of the few people he does trust.'

Ryan

Melanie wasn't home.

'She's out shopping with her mates,' said her Mum. 'She'll be so sorry to miss you, Ryan, especially after – anyway, we're all so pleased you're back safe and sound. He didn't hurt you, did he?'

'No, not at all, but I'm sorry I upset everyone. I didn't know he was planning to take me away.'

'Well, you're safe now, love, that's all that matters, isn't it?'

But it wasn't. He'd hurt all of them, Caroline, Philip, Lissie – and now Simon was mad at him, and he didn't think an apology was going to mend things with him. If he went for a long ride, didn't get back until dinner time, perhaps Simon would have calmed down. But when he arrived back at the farm, Simon was waiting at the gate for him. Ryan tried to push past him but Simon stood in his way.

'I owe you an apology,' he said. 'I shouldn't have yelled at you like that. I thought you were just making use of us, accepting presents like your new bike, and all the time you didn't care about any of us.'

'I didn't want to care! You care about people and they die or they hurt you or they abandon you.'

' I wish you'd told me about Joe and how he treated you.'

'I didn't want anyone to know. People treat you differently. They look at you, and they're sorry for you, perhaps, but they don't really want you in their gang – and then there are some who bully you because they know you're already a victim and you're not likely to fight back.'

Ryan was silent for a long time. And then he turned back to Simon.

'I wanted to be like you. I envied you, not being afraid of anything – and having all this.' He waved his hand towards the fields. 'Sometimes, when I wake up in the mornings, I wonder if it's all a dream, and when I open my eyes I'll be back in the room next to Joe's.'

'You should have told me all this,' said Simon. 'Twins should share things. I hope we can now."

Ryan turned away. His shoulders began to shake.

'Oh, for Pete's sake!' Simon sounded cross. 'Now you've got me crying too!'

Simon

It was the first time I'd cried for ages. The last time I'd blubbed, I think I was about ten years old. It was Christmas and Mum hadn't been able to get me numbers one, two and three on my long list of wants. I think she was between jobs at the time. I hadn't blubbed since, not even when she told me about Philip and that we'd be leaving London.

It was embarrassing. I told myself it was just a twin thing – crying in sympathy, something just physical. All the same, it was embarrassing and I left Ryan at the gate, scrubbed at my tears and went for a tramp round the fields before going back to the house. I hoped any evidence would be gone before Lissie saw me.

When I got back I saw we'd been besieged by the Press and TV again. Philip was furious, but nothing he did this time would budge them and we had to live with drawn blinds again. Although they were a nuisance, popping up from behind fences, trying to peer through windows, we did our best to ignore them, and eventually they went away.

I think all of us were happier in that last week of the holidays, and I could see that Mum was pleased Ryan and I were getting on so much better. Lissie approved too, and I think even Ryan was beginning to feel that we were one united, happy and safe family.

The last week of the holidays passed very quickly, and then we were putting on our new school uniforms, and getting out our bicycles for the ride to Redmond House. When we got there, I think every student was out in the playground, waiting for our arrival. It seemed we were famous, and they all wanted to be our friends.

Of course Lissie enjoyed being Queen of the Playground, but Ryan looked as if he wanted to turn round and cycle straight back to the farm. Me? I put on my best bored expression that said, What's all the fuss about? 'Ignore them,' I said, and flung my arm around his shoulders. And a day or two later, there was a new hot story in the local papers, our story was not even given a paragraph, and our new schoolteachers were keeping us on our toes with a very different approach to learning.

We didn't hear any more about our birth father. Ryan and I decided he'd left the country and perhaps was setting up his gallery in Carmel, just "*Oliver Daizley'*, without the *'And Son'* bit.

Except that a few weeks later, two huge parcels arrived. One for Ryan, one for me. Mine contained a case of the most expensive oil paints, artist quality, together with a range of brushes, and Ryan's contained a wooden box of several hundred artists' pastels.

There was no return address on either of them, and no message inside, but both of us knew who had sent them.

'These are fantastic,' I said to Ryan. 'How did he know I painted with oils?' Not that I cared, of course.

'I told him,' Ryan said, 'when we were painting together. I told him how brilliant you were at painting portraits – much better than me. I think he was quite sad he hadn't met you too.'

END

DID YOU ENJOY THIS BOOK?

If so, can you spare a moment to give it a star rating or write a brief review on Amazon? Thank you.

And here's an extract from The Boy Who Could Fly. This is the story of two boys and the circus. In Jamie Bird's dreams he is flying on a swing with long, long ropes, high, high in the sky. When he discovers that his great-uncle Sydney Bird, known as 'Una', was a famous trapeze artist, he knows this is what he wants to be. (Una is based on my own great-great-uncle, who tragically fell to his death in 1891 while performing. He was only sixteen.) Jamie's own story takes place in England during World War Two.

Jamie has run away to join a travelling circus, and this is the scene where he sneaks into the Big Top and climbs the ladder to the platforms 40 feet above the ground:

Early on the Monday morning, while the others were breakfasting, he sneaked into the Big Top. Empty and silent, all outside noises muffled by the thick canvas walls, the huge tent felt like a cathedral. He walked into the centre of the ring and stared up at the rigging that the Flying Giordanos had erected at daybreak. The maze of criss-crossed wires reminded him of the cat's cradle game Annie and Irene, the youngest Wibberleys, used to play.

The take-off platform and the four trapezes were right up there at the top of the rigging. Below them, some seven or eight feet above the ground, the safety net had been fastened. He thought about Una, who had had no safety net on the night he was killed.

'I'll be all right,' he told himself. 'Even if I fall, I won't hurt myself.'

All the same, he had to force himself to grasp the rope

ladder that stretched up and up and up to the take-off platform and begin to climb.

When he had watched the Flying Giordanos it had seemed so easy. And so quick. For Jamie it was painfully slow, and his fingers and the palms of his hands were beginning to hurt. It didn't help that the rope ladder swung in circles. What was he doing wrong? And then he remembered that none of the flyers climbed as if they were mounting an ordinary rigid ladder. They climbed by holding just one of the side ropes and pushing with their feet on the rungs to lever themselves upwards.

Of course Jamie had the wrong shoes, heavy laced up school shoes with stiff soles. No wonder he was finding it all so difficult. Perhaps he should give up and climb down again, before anyone saw him. But he was nearer to the take-off platform than to the ground. It made sense to carry on.

At last he reached the top of the ladder and found another problem. Getting off the ladder and on to the platform was another feat that had looked simple, but Jamie had to make several attempts before he managed it.

And then, sweating and trembling but proud of his achievement, he looked down.

The safety net that had given him such confidence now looked the size of a handkerchief. If he fell now he might miss it. *Would* miss it. He would miss it and die. Just like Una. Sick and dizzy, he felt himself swaying, felt his fingers loosening on the wires that held the platform.

Below, he could hear shouting. Mr Silver.

'What the hell d'you think you're doing? Get down here this minute!'

'I – I can't!'

Printed in Great Britain
by Amazon